What We Hold in Our Hands

short stories by

Kim Aubrey

DEMETER

DEMETER PRESS, BRADFORD, ONTARIO

Canada Council **Conseil des Arts**
for the Arts **du Canada**

The publisher gratefully acknowledges the support of the Canada Council for the Arts for its publishing program.

Demeter Press logo based on the sculpture "Demeter" by Maria-Luise Bodirsky <www.keramik-atelier.bodirsky.de>

Printed and Bound in Canada

Cover photo: Diane Aubrey

Library and Archives Canada Cataloguing in Publication

Aubrey, Kim, author
    What we hold in our hands: short stories / Kim Aubrey.

ISBN 978-1-927335-33-8

Cataloguing data available from Library and Archives Canada.

Demeter Press
140 Holland Street West
P. O. Box 13022
Bradford, ON L3Z 2Y5
Tel: (905) 775-9089
Email: info@demeterpress.org
Website: www.demeterpress.org

MIX
Paper from
responsible sources
FSC® C004071

for my parents

Contents

Over Our Heads

THE NOVEMBER I CELEBRATED MY NINETEENTH BIRTHDAY, I'd already been married a year and was living in a high-rise apartment near the university with my husband, Cam, and our baby daughter, Alice. That was twenty-five years ago, but I still remember how the sun slipped away from the living-room floor while we waited for Cam to return from his last class of the day, and how Alice would grab hold of my shirt or my long straight hair and hoist her body up, toes pushed into my thigh, face against my face, as she squealed and pointed at the china dolls banished to the top of the bookcase.

My mother had collected them for me on her antiquing expeditions in Southern Ontario and Northern New York State. Too bad she kept the dolls, whose dazed chalky faces used to give me nightmares, but threw out the superhero comics I'd loved to read, their strong black lines and simple flat colours constructing a world where help was only a page away.

If I didn't lift Alice to see the dolls, she'd try to climb onto my shoulders. As she strained upwards, I could see the long train of days stretching ahead, with me helping her to get the things she wanted, while my own dreams and desires receded into the distance. And I remembered staring at the "No Deep Dives" sign posted on the wall behind our high school pool, how the fine hairs on my arms used to rise and tug at my hungry skin, urging me to plunge in headfirst.

One day when Alice and I were out walking our familiar route along Bloor Street, she reached towards an empty paper cup on the sidewalk ahead, leaned forward in her stroller, and flexed her fingers wide as if she could see, taste, smell, and hear with them. Then, in one fluid movement, she dove out and struck the pavement.

I scooped her up. Her nose was bleeding and she was bawling. I started to wail with her, devastated at my failure to protect her. I'd buckled the strap that held her in, but must not have pulled it tight enough.

Pushing the empty stroller, I carried Alice to her doctor's office in the next block. Even living in the big city, our world was small, everything within walking distance, just like back home.

The doctor cleaned her face and said she was fine. The next day a violet bruise spread across the bridge of her nose, fading to a green smudge by the end of the week. When we went walking, people looked from Alice's nose to my face and tagged me as an irresponsible, or maybe even abusive, teenaged mother, like the ones you hear about on the news, who leave their toddlers alone overnight while they go dancing, or let them play next to twelve-storey-high open windows, or shake them until their brains are scrambled and they stop crying.

Whenever I heard those stories, I imagined a superhero swooping in to rescue, not only the babies, but the mothers too. By carrying them away from the scene of neglect and desperation, by setting them down on solid ground, she would somehow transform and restore them, leaving them better able to cope.

Cam and I were coping, keeping Alice safe and healthy. I cooked her chicken livers and brown rice. Cam stuck safety plugs into the electric outlets and made sure the windows and balcony door were always locked. I took Alice to every checkup and monitored the temperature of her bath water, never letting my eyes stray from her while she was in the tub. But often I cried from sheer exhaustion and longed to be transported to Paris or Vienna, where I imagined myself eating brioche and jam in an outdoor café while discussing books and art with dark-eyed, bearded men.

That November, as my birthday approached, and these day-dreams became more frequent, I discovered an Austrian café on Bloor Street where I could sit for half an hour with a cup of sweet coffee before Alice grew bored with her toys and the bites of pastry I offered as bribes. I watched her taste chocolate and almond paste for the first time, puzzlement, delight, or disgust blooming in her blue eyes. When she grew restless, I'd take her for long walks, window-shopping and browsing for books through the cool, dull, darkening afternoons.

It was on one of these walks that I saw a guy I'd known at home, a boyfriend of my older sister, Ellie. Alice had fallen asleep in her stroller, and I'd wheeled her into a bookstore out of the cold when I saw him. Jackson used to hang around our house or drive us into town where we'd watch a movie—my brothers and I sitting near the front while Jackson and Ellie sat in the back making out. You'd have thought Ellie would've been the one to get pregnant and marry young, not me. Back then, she never seemed to have a thought in her head that didn't involve boys or clothes. But now she was at teacher's college, sharing a house with a group of women who didn't shave their legs or wear deodorant, and here I was, a mother and wife, spritzing my wrists with free perfume every time I walked through the first floor of The Bay.

Jackson looked different from how I remembered him—sitting expressionless on our family's living-room couch, watching TV with Ellie wedged up against his side. Now he was reading a Penguin paperback, his face unshaven, brown hair long and wavy, tucked behind one ear so that he could see the page. He looked like any other university student in his heavy knit sweater, army pants, and running shoes, except more real and somehow larger than life, because he was from back home, and I hadn't expected to see him here.

Parking the stroller across the aisle, I picked up a book from the discount table, peering at him as I flipped through Joyce's *Dubliners*. Then, reading, I forgot about Jackson until I felt a hand on my back and looked up into his bloodshot eyes.

"Janelle? I thought it was you."

"I saw you reading, but I didn't want to disturb you."

I could smell the lemony perfume I'd sprayed on at The Bay and the mixture of cigarette smoke, marijuana, and perspiration escaping from his sweater. A pattern of X's crossed his chest over a pair of canoe paddles also crossed. I shook my head a little to make my dark hair ripple.

"I wrote a paper on Joyce's stories." He ducked his head and scratched his chin the way he used to when he was unsure of himself or talking to one of Ellie's lip-glossed girlfriends.

"I thought you were in Montreal," I said.

"Not anymore. I'm doing my Master's here."

I felt young and stupid, afraid to say the wrong thing.

"How's your sister?" he asked.

"She's at Western in teacher's college."

"Those days seem long ago, don't they, kid?" He always used to call me kid and ruffle my hair. His hand rose, then stopped.

"Do you want to go for coffee?" I asked, inspired by a vision of the two of us sitting in the Austrian café discussing books.

He frowned at Alice asleep in her stroller. "Will she be okay?"

My face grew hot. Alice hadn't figured in my café vision. Jackson must have heard about my pregnancy and marriage. When you're from a small town, you hear everyone's news whether you want to or not.

"She'll be okay for a while," I said, wondering whether he was concerned about Alice making a fuss in the restaurant or worried about her welfare—the smoky atmosphere, the adult conversations.

That was the beginning of my friendship with Jackson. I don't count the old days at home when I was just a kid, and he was the cool, cute boyfriend of my older sister, although Jackson claimed that even then he'd found me interesting.

"You used to ask the strangest questions out of the blue," he said later at the café, his fingers trailing across his beard. "And your eyes seemed full of knowing and of wanting to know."

"I used to study you, wondering what you were thinking," I said.

My coffee tasted especially sweet and bitter that day. Cam never said things like that about my eyes. He used to tell me I was beautiful, but now he never did. He was always busy. We both were, except that my busyness included a lot of hanging around with Alice, during which I could either tune out and daydream, or worry about my life—how much it had changed, how Cam was sometimes too tired to make love, how we weren't even twenty yet and we were like two old fogies sitting in front of the TV, watching other people pretend to live exciting, dramatic lives.

Already as I looked across the table at Jackson, I could foresee the potential soap-opera scenario of my life—handsome poet from her past sweeps Janelle off her feet. Her doctor husband suspects something, catches them together, and punches handsome poet in the jaw. Tears and apologies follow. The couple patch things up but the lover never disappears for long, returning in different guises, offering new temptations. I told myself I didn't want a part in that scenario, that what I wanted from Jackson wasn't sex so much as literature. He talked to me about Joyce's characters, how they were conflicted, loving Ireland but wanting to escape her. How Gabriel in "The Dead" suddenly sees himself as he is—coarse and compromised, unable to compete with the pure strong love of dead Michael Furey.

Alice slept in her stroller for an unprecedented hour and a half. When she woke, she stared at Jackson and bawled, going through stranger anxiety right on schedule, according to the Dr. Spock book my mother had given me. I lifted her, comforting myself with her warm body and hot tears. All through coffee, even though I'd told myself it wasn't what I wanted to happen, I'd longed to pull Jackson close, to feel his bristly face on my lips, his hot, sweet breath on my neck.

"We have to go," I said.

"Say hi to Cam for me." Cam's older brother, Dan, had been Jackson's best friend in high school. The smallness of our town used to make my bones ache to be out of there.

Friday and Saturday nights, Cam waited tables in a nearby restaurant while I stayed home, reading Alice stories from *The Richard Scary Omnibus* and splashing with her in the tub. I'd dry her plump body with a soft towel, rub her hair until it stood in curls, then dress her in a fuzzy cotton sleeper. After I'd nursed her, if she settled down to sleep in the crib beside our bed, I'd make myself a cup of tea and watch old movies until Cam got home, but if she fussed and whimpered, or screamed and screamed, her face growing redder by the minute, I'd become frantic not knowing how to help, begging her to stop, frightened by my growing desperation.

One such night, I bundled her into the stroller. As soon as we entered the dim hallway outside our apartment, her crying eased into hiccups. I walked her through the city streets to the restaurant where Cam was working. Holding her up to look through the window, we caught a glimpse of his tall figure in white shirt and maroon vest balancing plates of food over his head.

"Da Ba." Alice pointed at him, the first time she'd found a name for either of us.

"Yes," I said. "Daddy." I was in no hurry for her to call me Mama. I thought it would give her an added power over me. Now I know it was the separation I feared, how the knowledge that I was a person separate from herself might open the way to blame and resentment such as I'd felt for my own mother.

On our way there, I'd imagined sitting with Alice at an

empty table, eating a slice of apple tart while waiting for Cam
to finish, but all the tables were full and he was so busy that
I knew he wouldn't be happy to see us. As we watched him
disappear into the kitchen, I thought about Jackson, how we'd
lingered over coffee that afternoon while rain blurred the café
windows, and the sky darkened.

That night Cam arrived home exhausted and fell into bed
beside me, but I couldn't sleep. My chest was heavy with feelings I wished I didn't have, and I longed to cry like Alice until
my face was red and I woke the whole building.

Saturdays, I worked in the university library shelving books,
while Cam stayed home with Alice. I liked the earthy smell
of the stacks, where I rolled a cart from aisle to aisle, picking
up abandoned books on the way, stopping sometimes to pull
out a slim volume of poetry or a hefty history tome. I'd pass
a hand over their woven covers, slip my fingernail into the
close-pressed pages, flip them open, and read whatever words
presented themselves, as if they had something crucial to tell
me at that particular moment, like a friend who has to talk
to you right away.

Jackson and I didn't arrange to meet again. We simply hung
out in the same places. He looked for me at the library and
became a regular at the café, where he settled in for the afternoon with his books and papers. Alice liked to sit in his lap
and rub her hands across his rough cheek. I watched with envy,
imagined his beard scraping my own curious fingers. When she
grew tired of this, she'd climb up him to peer over the back
of the bench at the people in the next booth, charming them
with her gap-toothed smile. To win back her attention, Jackson
would draw faces on the tips of his fingers with a ballpoint pen,
moving them like puppets while he made noises that ranged
from a growl to a squeak.

During the winter, Alice learned to walk. I always knew it was
time to leave the café when I spent more time chasing her than

talking to Jackson. He never seemed to mind our clutter—the hats, scarves, mittens, juice bottles, toys, and storybooks—or the interruption to his writing and reading, or that when we ordered crêpes with jam and chocolate, Alice managed to smear all our faces with something sticky and sweet.

I pulled baby wipes from her diaper bag, handing one to Jackson, who dabbed at his beard, missing the orange jam stuck in the bristles.

"Here." I leaned across the empty plates, reclaimed the wipe, and carefully stroked the jam from his chin.

Cam spent most of his days in science labs, classes, or the library. When he could, he came home for lunch. He'd swoop up Alice and twirl her around. Or lift her onto his shoulders, galloping about the apartment, ducking at each doorway. As her head passed under the doorframe, her gleeful smile would shift to a brief worried suspension of breath, and I'd find myself holding my own breath, wondering if I'd been reflecting her worry, or if she'd caught mine.

Cam and I ate canned soup and grilled cheese while we watched the midday news, then reruns of *The Flintstones*. Our small table sat beside the kitchen, diagonally across from the television where Fred yelled for Wilma, who served up enormous slabs of ribs. Lulled by the cartoon's familiar sounds and images, we took turns opening blue-lidded jars and spooning strained carrots and pulverized chicken into Alice's eager mouth.

"I like it when you come home for lunch," I told Cam.

"Me too." He held out a finger for Alice to grab. His shaggy blond hair fanned out from walking through the wind. A too-small tan sweater stretched across his chest. Tiny holes had worn through the wool at the edge of the neckband and under the arms. When he smiled at Alice, his blue-grey eyes looked warm and tender like they used to when we were dating.

I draped my arms over Cam's shoulders, nuzzled his neck.

"That tickles, Janelle," he said, shaking me off.

"Let's sit on the couch for a while before you have to go back."

"What about Alice?"

"Alice is fine." I lifted her from the high chair, washed her face and hands, and set her down on the carpet to crawl. "Come on, Cam," I said.

He was standing, weight on the balls of his feet, staring out the big window as if ready to soar out and over the city. I reached my arms around his chest and squeezed. He lifted me so that my legs dangled.

"I wish you could spin me around like you do Alice."

"Your feet would hit the window and the shelves." He kissed me once on the lips before setting me down.

The way his eyes flitted past me, I could see his mind already clicking forward to the chemistry lab. I picked up Alice and held her close. She squirmed in my arms, reaching for Cam, who kissed her goodbye twice on each fat cheek.

When he left, she started to cry. She always cried when I went to my evening linguistics class or to work, but this was the first time she'd cried for Cam.

"Daddy will be back soon," I said, rocking her, offering a breast, unaware that, in a few years, she'd cry even harder, clinging to me as I left her at nursery school, screaming for a father she wouldn't see for months at a time.

As she settled down to nurse, I watched an unfamiliar soap on TV. A man and woman were kissing. She broke free, asking, "What about Jake?" The scene cut to Jake in the hospital listening through a stethoscope to a young boy's heartbeat, his furrowed brow expressing concern.

Alice's lips released their suction on my nipple, which pointed upward about an inch from her sleeping face. After carrying her to the crib, I took out my linguistics books, sat at the table, and began the assigned exercises. It was easy to label each syllable with its phonetic symbol, each word with its syntactical function—easy and boring. I turned on the radio, fiddling with the stations, stopping the dial when I heard Donna Summers' "MacArthur Park." I danced around the room, twirling and leaping like I used to in ballet, swaying and rocking during the slow parts. The song over, I stood by the window, heart pounding, and watched the people below until my breath and pulse slowed to normal.

I wondered what I'd be doing if I didn't have Alice, if Cam and I hadn't married. Would he and I be together? Would I have attended a different university? I'd planned to go to Mc-Gill to study English, improve my French, and write poetry in the coffee shops and delis of Montreal, to live on my own in practice for my dream of living and writing in a Paris *appartement*. But even having an apartment in a Toronto high-rise was exciting for Cam and me.

After a year, I still felt a thrill looking out the living-room window over the streets below. I'd place my hand on the cold glass, and peer at the scene through my fingers. An electric feeling would run down the back of my neck and along my arms. With this feeling came the thought that these must be someone else's fingers, that I must be living someone else's life, and somewhere out there was the person who was living mine—that woman in high-heeled boots striding up the side-walk, flinging open a restaurant door, or that man ducking his head against the wind, backpack slung over one shoulder, ignoring the traffic as he crossed the street.

On my birthday, my parents came to town, sleeping overnight on the pullout couch they'd bought us when we'd moved in. My mother gave me a new china doll, the first in years. She had curly brown hair, blank startled blue eyes, and a lacy pink dress.

"Thanks, Mom." I placed the doll on the shelf with the others.

"I thought she looked a bit like Alice."

I couldn't see any resemblance. If Alice got hold of the doll, she'd soon be smashed, her dress torn.

"How are you and Cam doing?" my father asked.

"We're fine," I said, thinking how I'd returned from work last Saturday to find Alice and Cam asleep on the couch, his head flung back while he snored gently, as if, even in his dreams, he was aware of her soft damp weight on his chest.

When Cam got home, my father patted him on the back, asking, "How's the old U of T?" My father, an alumnus, still thinks of those years before he became an accountant and married my mother, as the best of his life.

My mother simply nodded at Cam. She blamed him for taking me away, even though I would've gone farther east if I hadn't gotten pregnant and married him. When Cam and I separated two years later, her feelings about him changed. Like her, he became another person I had left behind.

Now, she sends Cam Christmas cards and calls him on his birthday. I've started to call him too. He's sweet and gruff with me, the coolness of many years gone from his voice. He tells me how Alice taught his sons to dive at their cottage on Lake Erie, how he sometimes cannot believe she's his daughter— she's so grown up, so sure of herself. She tells him about the play she's writing for her thesis, how she's learning to direct the student actors. She drags Cam and his wife to summer theatres, where, after half a lifetime of studied indifference to drama and literature, he admits to enjoying the plays.

"I want to do my Ph.D. in Montreal," Jackson said.

We were sipping coffee across from each other, while Alice banged my spoon against his *Collected Works of Milton*.

I started to daydream about living in Montreal with Jackson—the two of us strolling down tree-lined streets. Sometimes, Alice was there, running along beside us, pulling my hand to show me something in a shop window. Other times, it was just Jackson and me, bodies pressed together, eyes locked, oblivious to passersby. These fantasies became a secret addiction, a place I'd retreat whenever I felt lost or unhappy. If Cam arrived home when I was in the middle of one, or if Alice called me from her crib, I'd feel a stab of guilt over my eyes, would sometimes be blinded by it, unable to see clearly for moments afterward, staring up at Cam's distorted features or into Alice's blurry little face.

Looking back, I understand how wanting Jackson felt like a betrayal, not only of Alice and Cam, but also of myself. With my decision to give birth to Alice, instead of seeking an abortion, I'd appointed myself her champion, defending her right to exist in the face of pressure from our parents and friends, not to mention our own doubts and longings. In spite of all this opposition, or perhaps because of it, and thriving on it, I'd swooped down and saved Alice from non-existence. More than that, I'd grown her inside me and pushed her out into the world. But then came the hard part, the days and nights when I had to admit that I might not be up to the job, that the cape I'd donned might not be enough to separate me from the mothers I heard about on the news.

Afternoons in the café with Jackson helped me to cope. Daydreams helped too, by carving a space in the day where my stifled desires could take a few moments to stretch out and breathe.

In February, Jackson invited Cam and me to a party in his dorm.

"It'll be fun," he said. "I'll get to see you shake loose."

"We'll come if we can find a sitter," I said, knowing that with such short notice I wouldn't be able to find anyone I'd trust to take care of Alice.

When I told Cam, he said, "You go, Janelle. I'll stay with Alice. Jackson's your friend anyway."

"Okay, but I won't stay late."

"Stay as late as you want. Alice will be asleep, and I'll be studying. Enjoy yourself."

Cam pulled me to him and kissed me. He seemed to like the idea of my going out. I felt the familiar blinding pain seize my eyes.

But that night, I left Cam holding Alice and walked the few blocks to Jackson's dorm. Big, lazy snowflakes drifted down, but I felt warm in my winter coat and boots, comforted by the softness the snow lent the city, like blankets and pillows spread out on the street for a pyjama party. I stood outside Jackson's building for a while, gazing up as the flakes came faster. When I finally climbed the stairs to his room, my hair was wet with melt.

"Janelle." Jackson's eyes were bright and startled. "I didn't think you were coming." He took my coat, nodding and pacing, as if trying to remember where to put it.

"Sit down," he said, finally dropping it onto the bed in the corner. "No one's here yet."

Incense was burning on a shelf, Peter Gabriel playing on the turntable. I sank into a deep old armchair and stared at my feet in their grey woollen socks. Jackson, who sat cross-legged on the floor beside me with a bag of weed and some papers, started to roll a joint. I'd only smoked up once when I was in high school. Ellie used to call me a do-gooder, but when Cam and I were at one of his brother's parties a few weeks before graduation, Dan had given us a joint to share, saying, "This'll put you in the mood." That night we forgot about the condom in Cam's back pocket, and Alice was conceived.

Jackson offered me a drag.

"No thanks." I was determined not to go there again. "I'm nursing. The chemicals..."

"Sorry. Does it bother you if I smoke?"

"No. I like watching you." I'd noticed how Jackson's eyes got mellow back when he used to smoke with Dan in Cam's garage. It occurred to me that I'd been watching Jackson for years.

He held the joint in one hand and rubbed my sock-covered toes with the other.

"What's the snow like?" he asked after a long fragrant exhalation.

"Like wet velvet on my face. Or cats' tongues without the scratchiness."

"Let's go out and play in it." He squeezed my toes.

"What about the party?"

"I'll leave the door open. Ross will be here any minute. He just went to buy beer."

We walked to the park around the corner where we made snow angels and two giant snowballs from small ones we each rolled through the sticky snow. We scooped out the insides to make chairs, which we sat in, staring up at the sky.

"I feel like Gabriel Conroy watching the snow," Jackson said. "Separated from everyone and everything, yet connected too, by this big white blanket."

"Mmm," I agreed.

I never did go to the party. Jackson and I just stood outside his building for a while.

"I'm tired. I'm going home," I said, shivering in my snowy jeans.

He wrapped his arms around me. "I'm cold too," he admitted, holding me there. I was aware only of the warmth of our two bodies inside their winter coats, and his scent, an unruly mix of cinnamon, sawdust, and marijuana.

We stood like that until two guys yelled, "Hey, Jacks, where's the party?

"Bye, Janelle," Jackson called after me.

I took the long way home through the park where we'd played in the snow, and behind the big new library with its concrete ramp zigzagging up to the main floor. Then I passed the older university buildings, their stone ornaments shrouded with snow, the lamplight casting intricate patterns of light and dark, gold and grey onto their white lawns. I skirted Queen's Park full of shadowy trees, walked through Victoria College and under the archway onto St. Mary's Street, smiling at couples walking the snowy sidewalks and students tossing snowballs, but I didn't feel happy so much as grief-stricken and lost. Like Jackson, I felt alone too—cut off from the people I loved—but also bound up with them, carrying them everywhere.

When Alice was in grade school, she spent most of her summers with Cam. I'd write her long letters, marking the bottom of each page with rows of X's and O's, representing all the kisses and hugs I was unable to give her while she was away. The X's reminded me of the ones knitted into Jackson's old woollen sweater, how I used to stare at them when I was feeling too shy to look into his face.

In the spring, we didn't see as much of Jackson. We stopped frequenting the café because Alice wanted to be in the park or the playground, and Jackson was writing final papers for his courses. I still saw him at the library carrying stacks of books, dark circles under his eyes, his beard heavier than usual.

Cam was studying for exams, tense and troubled with night-mares of failure. He needed a high average for medical school, although the competition wasn't as fierce then as it is now. One evening during his study period, I told him that Jackson was coming to dinner.

"I'm not in the mood for Jackson." He picked up Alice's toys from the floor and dropped them into the playpen. "He reminds me of Dan, how Dan's still stuck at home working at the Canadian Tire, how that could be me if I don't do well on these exams."

"You'll do fine. You're smart, and you'll never be like Dan. And we're never moving back home."

"Yeah. We're never moving back home as long as your parents pay our rent."

"They like helping out," I said, filling a pot with water to boil the spaghetti. "What's the problem? As long as my parents can afford to help?"

"The problem is my parents can't, and it makes them feel

bad." He dumped Alice's blocks into the playpen where they rattled over the other toys like the rain that had pelted our windows the night before.

"So what do you want me to do about it?"

Cam just glared at me. Alice woke up crying. And the intercom buzzed.

He jabbed his finger against the red button.

I didn't know then that Cam *would* move back home for a couple of years, commuting to Waterloo where he'd be studying pharmacy, since his marks had not been high enough for med school. Or that I would have left for Montreal with Alice even before that, though not to be with Jackson.

In those days, I thought I had the power to make things happen just by saying or even thinking them. From childhood, I'd felt responsible for other people. My mother had leaned on me, confided her secrets, counting on me to help, since Ellie was so unreliable, and the boys were boys after all.

"You're the strong one, Janelle," she'd said. "I need you to make the boys dinner and keep them out of trouble."

"Why can't they get their own dinner?"

"I don't want them messing about in the kitchen, upsetting your father."

My father came home after my brothers and I had eaten. He patted my mother's head, brought her a cup of tea. "How's my darling?" he asked, holding her hand, playing with the fingers.

When I got pregnant, I'd felt confident that I could handle motherhood a whole lot better than my own mother had, that I could take care of Cam and Alice, keeping the three of us together, that I could give Cam so much love and support he'd make it through med school without a hitch.

While we waited for Jackson, I lifted Alice out of her crib and changed her soaking diaper.

"Mummum," she said, which meant she wanted to nurse. I heard the door open and Jackson's soft, eager voice in the hall. I longed to see him scratch his chin and to smell the exotic mix of scents rising from his sweater as I pressed my face briefly against his for a hello kiss. But I wasn't comfortable nursing Alice in front of him, and I didn't want to be stuck in my bedroom with her for the next half-hour.

"Mummum," she cried, tugging up my shirt.

"No," I said, pulling it back down. "Here." I grabbed one of Cam's old Matchbox cars from the top of the dresser to distract her. "Car," I said.

"Car," said Alice, clasping it to her chest while I carried her out to greet Jackson.

I reached to hug him with my free arm.

"What's that in Alice's mouth?" Cam yelled.

I pulled away from Jackson.

Alice's face was red, and she was choking. Something small, black, and round sat at the back of her mouth. Fishing it out with one finger, I found myself holding the saliva-soaked front wheels of Cam's Matchbox car. Held together by a metal axle, one wheel still bore its rubber tire, but the other was bare.

Cam snatched the wheels from me. "She must have swallowed the other tire." He grabbed Alice too.

"It won't hurt her," I said, hoping it was true. "It'll just come out the other end."

Alice was breathing again, but her eyes and mouth had narrowed, a sure sign she was about to bawl.

"You know she shouldn't play with those cars." Cam glared at me.

I retrieved the car from the floor, then threw it down the hall and into our bedroom where it rolled to a stop under the bed. My eyes started to burn. I knew that giving her the car had been wrong, that she could have been hurt, but my guilt only made me feel angrier and more resentful.

"The water's boiling." I headed for the kitchen as Alice began to cry.

"Can I help with anything?" asked Jackson.

"No."

Soon dinner was ready. My eyes still smarted, but Alice was squealing and running around the living room, bringing toys and books to Jackson, who sat on the couch joking about old times. Cam stretched on the floor, grinning, beer in hand. At dinner, Cam continued to reminisce. "Jacks, remember when you and Dan used to break into my locker and pinch my stuff?"

"Yeah, we loved to torment you. You were such a self-assured little creep."

"Remember when you took my coat and I had to walk home from school coatless, in a snowstorm. Boy, did Mom give it to Dan that time."

I thought Cam should be angry with Jackson for bullying him at school, but the two of them laughed like brothers, clutching each other's shoulders, while Alice slopped spaghetti around the tray of her highchair, her face orange with tomato sauce. Up on the top shelf, the row of china dolls gazed at the opposite wall, and I felt myself shift into that electric state I sometimes entered when looking out the window over our small patch of city.

"Janelle, what courses are you taking next year?" Jackson asked, just as I was imagining myself on a train, speeding eastward along the curve of Lake Ontario, watching the city shrink.

"I haven't thought yet." I stared at the gold bristles on his chin.

"I can help with your choices." He twisted the last strands of spaghetti onto his fork.

"Maybe I won't take any courses next year. Maybe I'll get a full-time job or go to community college and learn something useful like book-keeping."

"Don't be stupid," Cam said. "You're not giving up your education. Having a baby is not going to change our lives."

"But it has changed our lives. We're different already. We don't live like normal students, like Jackson, who can goof off when he wants and spend the afternoon drinking coffee and talking to Alice and me. You work constantly, either studying or waiting tables, and I'm attached at the breast to Alice. Even if I put her in daycare, she'd still be on my mind all day." My eyes were hot with tears. "I'm a mother now and I can't shake that, just like I can't shake the thought that if you don't do well on your exams you'll blame Alice and me for distracting you."

I jumped up from the table to get a tissue. Jackson and Cam stared at their plates, but I didn't feel the least bit embarrassed or regretful for my outburst. Maybe it was the talk about the old days that had gotten to me, how hilarious Cam now found the bullying he'd suffered from his brother and Jackson, like those days were fun compared to what he was enduring now, tied to Alice and me.

I grabbed the dishcloth from the kitchen sink, swabbing Alice's face and hands. As I lifted her from the highchair, she wrapped her fingers around a chunk of my hair and pulled. I pried open her fist, handed her over to Cam.

"I'm going for a walk." I poured apple juice into one of Alice's cups. "Give her this. I'll be back in an hour so you can study."

"I'll come with you," said Jackson.

"No, you stay here and help Cam with the dishes."

I shut the door, muffling Alice's cries, taking refuge in the quiet hallway with its evening smells of hot oil, cumin, and cardamom.

Whenever I eat Indian food, which is one of my favourites, I feel a pleasant ache in my chest for those days in the high-rise with Cam. I imagine him in his suburban house, fixing a leaky tap, hanging pictures with his wife, or helping his two boys with their homework. Sometimes I even call him, and his voice sounds reassuringly altered, the voice of a middle-aged man who carries the ghost of his younger self lightly, like a baby on his shoulders.

Cam has become a parent again with the chance to do things differently, a risk I haven't taken, an opportunity I have not allowed myself, relieved at how well Alice has managed, and how little she resents me. When she assures me that I'm a good mom and wraps her strong swimmer's arms around me, I want to tell her that it's not true, that she deserved better, but I know I'm still holding myself to an impossible standard. Outside, the air was fresh and warm for April. A fine mist like some early mornings back home hung over the city streets. I walked through the campus, past the library to the Athletic Centre, remembering the night of Jackson's party, missing the snow.

In Montreal, eight years later, I would run into Jackson in the library, his familiar long face strangely beardless, looming over the periodicals. I was a grad student at McGill, and he was an assistant professor at Concordia, but he ducked his head, stammering his way through our conversation.

"I often think of those days in the café," he said, clutching a magazine.

But just when I thought we might become lovers, I met a man who taught with Jackson and would become my second husband, who said to me at a party, "When it snows, I always want to order Chinese food. And when it rains, I have to look at old comics. I keep a pile beside my bed and under my desk. Superman, Spiderman, the Hulk..."

I peered through the windows of the Athletic Center. The swimming pool wasn't busy so I went inside, showing my student card at the door to the women's locker room. A girl who looked about my age was pulling on a bathing suit. I took off my sweater. Under my T-shirt, my breasts were big with milk, but they weren't leaking, and my belly had slimmed down over the winter. No one would guess I was a mother.

As I pushed open the door to the pool, a chlorine-scented steam settled over me. At the far end, a woman was teaching four young girls to dive. I sat on a bench and watched each one climb the steps of the diving board, run, bounce off the end, and slice the water with her outstretched arms, feet flailing above. My own bare arms tingled from the rush of bubbles I imagined the girls must feel, bubbles that stir the surface of their skin, before rising overhead, and away.

Eating Water

WHEN I WAS A TODDLER, MY MOTHER USED TO CROSS THE straps of my gingham overalls twice—once over my back and once across my chest. I was so small, so slight, a breeze could have swept me away. A hurricane was overkill.

The big wave rises and curls. I stand near the surf, small legs planted in the sand, wearing the crossed-in-front overalls with the legs rolled up past my pointy knees. My father has persuaded my mother into celebrating his birthday with a picnic on the beach, even though the radio weatherman has called for afternoon storms associated with Hurricane Arlene. The weatherman does not expect Arlene herself to visit the island, only her entourage of winds and rains. No need to put up the hurricane shutters or fill the tub with water. The mere twenty square miles of rock, sand, and soil that make up our hook-shaped island will be safe from Arlene's bright, quietly cunning eye.

Were my parents downright negligent or merely foolish? I can see my father lounging on the woollen blanket they bought in Canada on their honeymoon, my mother posing between him and me on the beach, the palms fanning and the bay grapes bursting behind her. Her blonde hair is brushed up into a beehive, and she wears a sundress, sewn from the same pink gingham as my overalls, with a little white cardigan shrugged over it. I don't know if these are memories or imaginings. As I've spent most of my life watching my parents carry on, it seems not unlikely that even before I reached the defiant age of two, I was already taking notes on their expressions and apparel. How they dressed like actors playing parts in a television family. He in his tipped fedora and pale grey flannels, the waistband snug around his belly, the striped suspenders a mere accessory. She in her bright, starched frocks, a fresh hibiscus pinned to her hair. How they paraded their love with handholding and lustful glances, how he stared into her eyes before anointing her hand with a kiss.

My parents lie together on their big blanket, lips locked. My mother sends me guilty sideways looks before standing to brush the sand from her skirt. The sun sneaks through the clouds, blessing my hair with a splash of light. She rummages in her straw bag for the camera. My mouth gapes wide in a jack-o-lantern grin. You can see the thick black wave rolled tight behind me like an enormous Persian rug.

After that day on the beach, I started to bulk up. My skimpy toddler body, now alert to the dangers of smallness and lightness, incorporated this new knowledge into all of its smart little cells, which set to work building fat. I'd only to watch my father to learn how it was done. Every day he padded himself against life, seeking comfort for his failures in French toast and syrup, bacon and tomato sandwiches, the yellow cookies he bought by the boxful from the Bermuda Bakery, strands of black and red licorice his sales girls fetched him from the candy store. By the time I was ten, I knew all his secrets, could smell sweets on his breath, identify the crumbs on his necktie and in the creases of his shirts, could recognize in his brown eyes fear disguised as revulsion whenever he was unable to avoid looking at me, his young and female mirror image.

Spray from the surf tickles the nape of my neck. Sand dissolves under my feet as the surf pulls me back, and a dark wall of water rises. Salt burns nose, throat, and eyes. I am swallowed whole and alive, reclaimed by the sea.

In Junior Four science class, Miss Reese told us that all life on earth evolved from the sea. Jane Pemberly raised her hand, sticky from the jujubes hidden in her desk.

"God created Adam and Eve," she said, a piece of jujube stuck to her tooth making her lisp. "They didn't come from fith. It thays tho in the bible."

"The bible says the waters were here first," countered smart and tactful Miss Reese. "Fish came before birds and animals. Everything originated in the water. Susan, please stop kicking Jane's chair." But Jane deserved it, spouting Sunday school propaganda. I hadn't believed a thing they'd taught us there, the teachers passing out pictures of bible stories for us to colour, while they nodded over morning coffees and checked their makeup in sneaky compacts.

I believed that the sea had been trying to take me back, and it would have succeeded if my mother hadn't been such a strong swimmer—a good Ontario girl who grew up beside the lake, swimming and rowing.

Off comes her little white sweater. Off the gingham dress. Into the sea she runs, diving after me where the beach drops off into deep water.

My mother was a queen, an Amazon, a beauty. She tied herself to my father with a thick scratchy rope they both called "love," the kind of rope that hung from the ceiling in my school's gym, a big knot tied at the bottom. Some girls could shinny up that rope no problem, but all I could do was hang on, dangling back and forth like the clapper of a bell or the weight of a cuckoo clock.

I reached both hands up the rope as far as they would go, and pulled hopelessly, begging time to hurry me past the torture of gym class and all the other classes to come.

"Fatty Fatty Fatso," whispered Jane Pemberly from a few feet away.

I stuck out a leg to see whether I could kick her in the face. Maybe. But how to make it look like an accident? I leaned my weight to one side then the other, swinging farther out, back and forth. The girls cleared a space around me. I was flying, spinning in a wonky circle. The gym teacher tried to grab the rope, but had to jump away when the bulk of me came barrelling towards her.

"Stop that this instant, Susan. Just you stop that!"

"I can't," I yelled. "I don't know how." I was crying already, thinking how I would be teased for this.

Some of the girls screamed, "Stop, stop," while others yelled, "Go, Fatty, go."

Watching their wild faces swing by, I grew calmer. The thick gym mats lay below me. All I had to do was to let go and fall, but I wanted to make a heroic gesture, to leap and land standing on the leather horse several feet away. I could see myself tossing a cape over one shoulder like Zorro. As I swung close to Jane and her friends, I released the rope and cast myself in their direction, knocking over Mary Bright, a tall girl who usually stayed out of my way. She fell against Jane, causing the whole class to tumble onto the mats, more of a psychological domino effect than a real one. Everyone was laughing or crying. I chose to cry, which is probably why they hated me. If you're fat, they expect you to be jolly.

I had decided to hate school when my mother first left me there alone, staring at the green snot that oozed from Jane Pemberly's nose, while the kindergarten teacher said, "Susan, would you please go to the end of the line," because I hadn't known the protocol and had stood facing Jane in the teacher's place at front. Walking past the other girls, observing their pale hair and slim freckled limbs, their blank, sullen, or friendly faces, I took notes on how different I was. They belonged to the same tribe as my mother—the blonde, pale, and thin—while I had my father's black hair and deeply tanned Mediterranean skin, his round barrel belly.

What I failed to notice was the absence of brown faces in the line. I'd yet to learn the word, "segregation," or that the teasing and targeting I was about to experience were not the same as outright exclusion.

"How did you like school?" my mother asked.

"There's an orange fish in a bowl and paste for gluing pictures," I said, choosing not to mention the helpless disgust I'd endured, staring at Jane's crusty nose all day. The teacher had made us partners, which meant we'd had to sit together, and hold hands on the way to lunch. Neither did I mention the shame I'd felt every time I did something wrong, like tasting the smooth milky glue or slapping Jane's hand away while we said grace. I didn't want my mother to think I was one of those difficult children she complained of at the boys' school where she taught art and gym.

I don't know where I'll end up—waving whitely underwater like a shipwrecked captain, my overall straps snagged on a coral fan, or floating free with a fish's tail and a mermaid's flowing hair. Or in my mother's arms, warmed and revived, returned from the dead.

One day in science class, Miss Reese told us about hurricanes, how the warmer the air, the more pressure and speed they could build. How it wasn't fair that they were all named after women. While she talked, I could smell the salty, sulphurous ocean, and feel the wave wrap around me, stealing my breath.

"Susan, are you okay?" Miss Reese's voice seemed to enter my ears through the echoing cavern of a conch shell. "You're white as a ghost," she said. "Jane, take her to sick bay."

Jane grabbed my hand, yanking me from my chair. My legs shook, and my ears still hummed with the conch's swirling sound.

My mother's strong, warm hands grip my ankles. She pulls one way, while the ocean pulls the other, a tug-of-war over my young, vulnerable bones and slight, soft flesh. My lungs fill with water.

Legs wobbling, I leaned against Jane's sturdy shoulder.

"If you're faking..." she hissed into my echoing ear.

In sickbay, the nurse stuck a thermometer into my mouth and wrapped a blood pressure cuff around my arm. Jane stood watching. If I was sick, she'd be the one to divulge the details at recess, everyone leaning in close. If I wasn't sick, she'd tell that too, after she pushed me around for a while at the edge of the playing field.

The nurse pressed the cold face of a stethoscope against my skin. "Back to class with you," she told Jane.

Calling my mother at work, she said, "Susan has a fever and her chest sounds full." Then, dangling the stethoscope from one finger, "I suppose she can rest here for the afternoon, but she should see a doctor as soon as possible."

The doctor said I had pneumonia.

"How long will she have to stay home?" my mother asked.

I knew she was thinking of the days she'd miss at work. She had little patience for illness. Only my father could interrupt the proper pace of her days with impunity.

The pain in my chest eased a little at the prospect of missing school, but after a few days at home, I languished in bed, wondering what games Jane and her friends were playing at recess, and what new marvels of science Miss Reese had disclosed.

As much as I claim to have hated school, I felt acknowledged there. The teachers could be counted on to yell at me or send me to the office, the girls relied on to tease me and sneak mouldy sandwiches into my desk. The bells always rang on time, the days ended, and, after some name-calling or shunning at the bus stop, I found my way home, where I was, for the most part, left alone.

My parents never took me to the beach again, although I went there with my grandparents whenever they visited from Canada. My mother and father were either working or immersed in bottomless talks about his business woes. Throughout my childhood, he started one business after another while the money he'd inherited from his parents swirled away. He sold Persian rugs imported from a distributor in New York, but the prices he had to charge were too high and the demand on the island too small. He tried his hand at T-shirts and souvenirs, but could not withstand the fierce and entrenched competition. He thought the restaurant business might be his calling, but he was too ambitious—linen tablecloths, French waiters, steaks imported fresh from Alberta, white asparagus from Belgium.

One Sunday when I was ten, my parents occupied a bench in the Botanical Gardens, jawing over my father's failing souvenir store, while I chased peacocks, which flew to the top of the arbour and teased me with hints of turquoise and indigo. I rested on a wall a few feet away from an anole doing pushups on the limestone, its green skin darkening to blend in with the grey wall. While I was distracted by the lizard, one peacock unfurled his splendid feathers and darted at me. All those bright blue eyes. I turned to check if my parents had been watching, but they'd strolled over to the rose garden, their heads bent over some new variety. A triangle of blood bloomed on my wrist.

"The peacock bit me," I cried, waving my wounded arm.

My mother waved back. My father sniffed a rose.

"It hurts," I yelled.

My mother looked at my father, as if for permission, before striding towards me.

"What happened?" she asked, pulling the white scarf from her hair to wrap around the bite.

"A peacock did it." I threw my arms around her neck, glancing over her shoulder at my father, who was kicking the gravel path, clouds of dust rising from his newly polished shoes.

My mother reaches one hand for my sinking head, while the other clings to my leg. Scooping me to her chest, she swims on her back, kicking against the tide, holding my face up to the fresh rain.

I'd always wanted her to love me best. She'd saved my life with heroic flair, allowing me almost to forget her part in exposing me to the danger. My father often called her a "magnificent creature." That was how she appeared to me too—an exotic, lovely bird who did not belong with my short, stout, heedless dad.

Saturdays, I helped in his souvenir store, counting money, calculating profit margins on items such as ice cream cones, seashell necklaces, and coconuts carved to look like heads with fake wooden cigarettes hanging from their mouths. For a ten year old, I had a precocious interest in how to run a business. Miss Reese, worn down by my repeated questions about profit and loss, had given the class a lecture on economics, calling it "the other science."

"Dad," I asked. "Wouldn't you make more money if you bought these things directly from the manufacturer?"

He stared blankly, and waved me away from the cash register.

"When I'm older, can I manage the store for you?"

"You'll have to lose some weight."

"You're fatter than me," I said.

He looked past me at the bikinis tied onto cardboard cutouts of women's bodies with slim waists and curving hips. "Looks are important for girls."

"What about Mrs. Trott?" I asked. Mrs. Trott worked at the store during the week. She was a large, round black woman who always gave me peppermints and asked how my mother was.

"It's different for her," he said, but would not explain why.

Not for the first time, I found myself wishing I had brown skin. It seemed a kind of camouflage that would allow me to blend in with the island, to really belong here, to be welcomed by the ladies at the bus stop who greeted each other with jokes and laughter, who scolded and worried over the black children, tidy and polite in their beige or maroon uniforms, but whose faces zipped shut when I tried to smile at them or say hello.

"It's not my fault I take after you," I said, shaking out the picked-over T-shirts, folding them smooth again the way Mrs. Trott had shown me.

When the store failed, I wondered if it was because my father was fat, if looks were important for men too.

At school one morning, Jane Pemberly pulled my chair from

under me, as I was about to sit down. Pain wormed up my back. Laughter ratcheted through the class.

"You broke my tailbone," I accused her.

"Sissy," she muttered.

The nurse said I was fine. I told my mother I fell off a swing during recess. She gave me an aspirin as she ran the bath.

"Turn off the taps when the tub's full." She grabbed her purse on her way out to meet my father for dinner in town.

I lay floating in the warm water, listening to it lap over the sides of the tub. I knew I'd filled it too full, only turning off the taps when the water was a couple of inches from the edge. I imagined myself slipping on the wet floor and really breaking my tailbone, like my father had done when he and my mother were first married and deliriously happy, before I was born. What if I fell asleep in the bath and drowned?

My mother lays me flat on the blanket, pushes my stomach to make the water spurt from my lungs, then presses her lips to mine. I feel life come sucking back on the wave of her breath. I will not be a mermaid or a dead captain. I'll be a living girl, exposed to the whole, damned, painful arc of life yet to come.

By the time my parents arrived home, I'd dried the floor with fresh towels and fallen asleep, my hair damp on the pillow.

In the morning, Jane called.

"Are you okay?" she asked.

"Yes. No thanks to you."

"Just checking," she said before hanging up.

In the years that followed, a strange new camaraderie would sometimes rise amongst the girls in my class, and I'd be pulled along inside of it, as we walked to the bus stop during a storm, jostling and joking with each other, or jumped into someone's pool at a party after sharing an illicit bottle of strawberry wine. As we grew older, cruelty went underground, and tolerance surfaced. Maybe it helped that the government cracked down on segregation, forcing our school to admit African-Bermudian girls. Three joined our class. No one teased them or refused to invite them to parties, but Dina, Janette, and Joan formed their own group and, except for the occasional inclusion of Jane Pemberly, kept mostly to themselves. I did too, my weekends often spent in the Botanical Gardens, where I read novels, examined the insides of flowers, or watched the anoles blend into a branch or a stone, and where I was always careful to avoid the peacocks.

The day after my fifteenth birthday, Jane Pemberly brought a cupcake to school for me—yellow cake with white icing and a pink candy rose.

"What's wrong with it?" I asked.

"Nothing." Jane twisted her freckled face into what appeared to be a smile. "We had cupcakes for my brother's birthday, and I thought you should have one, since you just had a birthday too."

I didn't know whether to trust Jane, but the cupcake looked too good to pass up—sweet vanilla icing, fresh crumbly cake. I ate the whole thing, offering her the rose to be polite. She popped it into her pink mouth. After that, we became friends.

Jane said, "We've always been friends. We used to play on the swings in kindergarten."

"You threw the swings at me, or pulled on my ankles when I was swinging. I don't call that friendly."

"Well, you always made me laugh. You were so funny. That time on the rope in gym class. I nearly died."

So Jane and I were friends, whether we always had been or not. We paraded through town Saturday afternoons, our long hair—hers red, mine black—gleaming from a hundred brush strokes, our skin deeply tanned from sitting slathered in baby oil, our big, early-developed breasts squeezed into tank tops or sweaters. Jane liked a young sous-chef my father had hired for his failing restaurant, so we often stopped by to say hello. My father grunted at us, but the sous-chef always smiled, taking a break from his chopping and stirring to chat. We hungrily kissed boys in the dark of the Rosebank and Island cinemas, while they groped for our breasts with hot, damp hands. Or we took the bus to the beach, where we bodysurfed in the warm, salty water, waiting for big waves.

At first, Jane had to coax me. She found a Styrofoam board for me to float on, assured me that the ocean was calm, showed me how fun it could be to splash in the surf and to let the water carry you. When I finally ventured in, the sun warmed my back. Waves rose and fell beneath the board, lulling the fear from my limbs. My arms, crossed on top of the Styrofoam, felt sturdy and strong, nothing like the short, skinny arms that had flailed in this ocean fourteen years ago.

The rain comes harder. Great drops pelt our heads, soak the uneaten sandwiches. Waves crash up the beach, splash my parents' feet. Wearing only a wet slip, my mother bundles me in the woollen blanket, shouts at my father to grab the picnic basket, then runs for the car, clutching me in her arms, as the surf swallows her gingham dress, and Arlene's eye looms closer.

In the summer, Jane and I found jobs together at a jewellery store, where we sold Bermuda charms and bought each other gold hoop earrings with the commissions we earned. After work, sporting our new earrings, we walked to the bus stop.

"You look like a gypsy," she said, pushing her hair behind her ears.

"You look like a hooker." I laughed as she tried to shove me into the road. "You're not strong enough to budge me."

"Oh yeah?" She grabbed my hand and yanked me off the sidewalk. Together we knocked over a parked moped.

"I'm pretty strong," she said.

Jane wasn't as big as I was, but she was chunky with muscle from playing softball and tennis, and she liked to eat. In the fall, we got lunch passes to walk into town where we'd buy burgers, fries, and half a dozen cream puffs from the bakery. Jane still kept a bag of jujubes in her desk, tossing them to me across the room when the teacher's back was turned.

The two of us graduated from high school in long black dresses. The other white girls wore colours named for flavours of sherbet—pineapple, raspberry, lime. Mary Bright, in long yellow silk—like a lemon popsicle—said we looked slutty, so we adjusted our bras to show more cleavage, and talked up the tattoos we planned to get on our trip to New York at the end of summer. We'd be attending different universities, each about an hour's drive from Manhattan.

After the ceremony, which took place in the evening at one of the hotels, Jane grabbed Dina and Joan, and the four of us shared a joint beside the pool. Joan wore a bronze-coloured sheath, which glistened in the moonlight. Dina's dress was a deep purple that seemed to absorb the night.

"I like your dress," I told Dina.

"I like your rose."

"Thanks." I touched the coral rose I'd forgotten was pinned to the narrow strap of my dress.

"How is it that four gorgeous queens like us don't have dates?" Jane asked.

"Dina and I have dates," Joan said. "We just didn't see dragging them to this thing." She flicked a hand towards the lit and unlit windows of the hotel, as if flinging away something she'd put up with, but no longer needed.

My head felt light and drifty. I started to laugh, and wouldn't stop until Jane splashed me with pool water.

My parents hadn't made it to the graduation. My father hardly went anywhere since he'd had to close the restaurant. My mother said he was collecting himself.

"The graduation dinner would be too much. He'd sit there convinced that everyone was whispering about him."

"Why can't *you* come?" I hadn't told her I was getting a science award.

She blinked her blue eyes twice. "I can't leave him alone right now."

The evening of the ceremony, as I'd waited outside the house for Jane, my father had lumbered up the garden steps, carrying a handful of roses.

Squinting in the sunlight, he'd said, "You look nice."

I'd almost fallen off my platform shoes.

"You have your mother's smile. I never noticed before."

"You never *look* at me."

Now that he was finally giving me an ounce of admiring attention, I allowed the anger lurking in my cells to spread through me, making me feel powerful, clearing my head. I'd been trying so hard to win my mother's love with a show of independence and resiliency that I'd managed to ignore how sometimes my father had seemed as hostile as the girls at school, and how other times his indifference had made me feel as lost and worthless as a mermaid on dry land.

Arlene is by no means the worst hurricane to hit the island, but, in spite of the weatherman's assurances, she does hit us squarely with eighty-five-mile-an-hour winds. At home, my father struggles to put up the storm shutters in the pelting rain, but gives in after covering only the front of the house. Unfortunately, the wind is blowing against the back. In the night, a branch smashes my bedroom window. I wake in my crib, and watch broken glass twinkle in the glow of the nightlight, while the wind shoots my pink gingham curtains straight across the room.

Jane and I left the graduation dance early and rode our mopeds to the beach, where we sat on the sand in our long dresses. The air felt soft and salty, the darkness thick and comforting as a blanket. Invisible out there on the moonless Atlantic, cruise ships, freighters, and sailboats were daring the crossing. I told Jane how the sea had almost reclaimed me. My voice sounded faint and lost against the surf's rhythmic rush, but Jane's laughter rang out, filling my ears.

"Hurricane Susan, are you afraid a wave might steal you back to your sea mother?" She tugged my hair, making the tops of my shoulders tingle.

"Stop that." I shook my head, but the feeling wouldn't shift.

"*I'm* afraid," she whispered. Her hand crept into mine and settled there. This time I didn't slap it away. Instead I let the warmth rise up my arm and into my lungs, like the crest of a wave.

Earlier, in the garden, my father had handed me one coral-coloured rose. "The rest are for your mother."

I'd been prepared to stomp on the rose with my chunky heel when he sighed,

"This time, I've gone under," and I saw that the fear and disappointment in his eyes had nothing to do with me.

As my mother dashes to save me, my father notices the nasty chop out past the reefs and the unnatural darkness of the noon sky. He shouts after her, "Be careful! Don't go in too deep!" Perhaps he even runs down the beach and grabs at her arms to stop her, yelling at her to get out, afraid he'll lose her—his anchor, his lifeline. The rain begins to fall then and causes him to look up, loosening his hold, as he opens his mouth for the first gentle drops, briefly comforted for any loss he might suffer by the sweet water that begins to fill his mouth.

Unfinished

"HALF ROOM"

Four glass keys hang in a Plexiglas box in the YES *Yoko Ono* exhibit, the light striking each curved handle on a slightly different plane. They remind Ann of icicles or transparent candies. She wants to break into the box and hold one in her hand. She imagines a great glass door coaxed open with one of these keys, making available what she has always longed for, but denied herself.

A green apple sits on a white column. Someone has taken a bite, exposing the white flesh, which has turned a little brown, like lightly toasted bread. Ann wants to eat from the apple but worries what the people standing behind her might think.

Pieces of broken bottle glass lie in a case, each labelled with a different date. They represent mornings for sale, lenses for looking at and transforming the sky. The dates are mostly past now, but at the time of their original exhibit some thirty years ago, they were future dates for the purchase of future mornings, like promises or party invitations, crisp and bright with hope. She'd thought those old mornings were gone, but here they are, captured in this showcase. She cannot reconstruct the mornings, which continue to blend into one another—all those glasses of orange juice and bowls of oatmeal, the distracted kiss at the door as her husband escaped early to work, the kids' last-minute scurry for books and shoes, the purgatorial round of carpools. She has no desire to examine them through these bits of broken glass, keen reminders that both of her children have left home, that Duncan, her youngest, has almost finished his first year of university in a small city one-hundred-and-sixty miles away, where he's looking for an apartment.

An accordion book stretches across one wall. Its pages dance with dashes of black ink. In the wide broken strokes, she sees people and animals, faces, movement, lines shaky with laughter. From one black splotch, a woman's face emerges—eyes closed, mouth held open in a yawn or a scream.

In the next room, she finds herself drawn to an exhibit in which everything is cut in half and painted white. She tries to conjure the absent halves. Half a chair. Half a painting. Half a teapot. She summons the phantom half of the empty sawn-off suitcase, the piece that would make it whole and useful, so that someone could pack it full of clothes for a trip. She tries to imagine where that someone would go.

The phone rings behind her. She turns and reads the sign posted beside it, then grabs for the receiver because people are approaching, and because the sign says, "If the phone rings, pick it up and talk to Yoko."

"Hello," she says in the crisp, daunting voice she uses to answer the phone in her husband's dental office two days a week.

"Hello?" says a woman who sounds exactly as she imagines Yoko would sound—a small but powerful voice, ageless, with a still distinct Japanese cadence. "Are you enjoying the show?"

"I love the show," Ann gushes.

"I love you!" Yoko says.

"Oh," she gasps, and then, "I want a glass key."

"Take one."

"I couldn't."

"That's too bad." Yoko sounds disappointed, but adds brightly, "Enjoy the rest of the show."

"Wait," she says, but Yoko has already hung up. She'd wanted to ask her what it all meant.

Ann stares at some framed scraps of paper, reads the explanation on its small plaque, but the only part that registers is a quote from Yoko, saying, "Nine is a spiritual number, meaning 'unfinished.'" Then she knows what she has to do—return to the exhibit eight more times. It will be a kind of mission, to unearth what lies hidden here, to await Yoko's next phone call.

DAY TWO. "CUT PIECE"

In the video, Yoko sits on stage while people walk up from the audience to cut pieces from her black dress. Her shoulders rise and fall dramatically as the participants approach her with sharp scissors, and bear off bits of fabric, stuffing them into pockets or abandoning them on the stage. The dress is disappearing. Some cutters are tentative, taking small swatches, mementos. Others wish to expose her bare skin. One man leaves her clutching her arms to her chest, bra straps snipped, slip pared away, breathing hard. Ann finds her own breath quickening. Her arms cross her chest, one hand gripping each shoulder.

She wonders at Yoko's devotion to her art, her willingness to sacrifice comfort and peace of mind to men and women with scissors. Ann has sacrificed her time, her comfort, and her happiness, but never for art. She has tolerated the relentless drilling in her husband's white office as she sat by the phone writing up appointments and bills. She has endured countless committee meetings, bent forward taking minutes, her sharp pen scratching the paper as it ran out of ink. She has nervously pushed shears across the tender napes of her children's necks, trimming their soft brown hair.

DAY THREE. "PAINTING UNTIL IT BECOMES MARBLE"

This is part of a series of instructional "paintings" or instructions for paintings. They are written in Japanese characters, framed in two rows covering one wall of the first room. Next to each painting sits a stack of cards with translations in French and English. The cards are meant to be collected, read, and the instructions followed so that everyone can make art. This one instructs Ann to frame a painting, then let visitors cut out their favourite parts, or blacken them with ink. Does Yoko mean that the painting will become like marble, shot with veins of mineral, swirls of light and dark, absence and presence, like the room where everything is cut in half? Does she mean that it becomes more solid as it disappears? That nothing ever really vanishes? Those stolen or erased pieces still offer their ghostly support, their clues to meaning.

Hearing the phone ring in the next room, she runs for it. Too late. A young woman in a neat black suit has picked up the receiver. Ann stands a few feet away, pretends to look at the sawn-in-half chair, trying to listen to the woman's side of the conversation. A group of teenagers troops by, laughing and pushing each other, scattering into smaller groups and pairs. One slouching boy with his hands deep in his pockets reminds her of Duncan last year, walking out the door with his friends at night, ducking his head as she told him to drive carefully. Now she wishes he dared to be less careful. He's a gifted tenor who loves music, but he's followed his father's advice and is majoring in science in preparation for dental school.

By the time the teenagers have dispersed, the woman in the suit is gone. Ann imagines her tidy outline fading into the exhibit.

DAY FOUR. "WALL OF DOODLES"

She counts seventy-two framed pen-and-ink drawings, each consisting of tiny black dots, which make up an abstract image. The sign says that Yoko drew them as part of her daily routine, often while talking on the telephone. Was she drawing one when she called the gallery a few days ago? Ann wonders if she could amass a similar collection of images if she saved her phone doodles. Is that all it takes to make art? Valuing one's daily productions?

She used to know how to do it, when she was in school and university, even when she was first married. She'd just finished a BA in art history and was working as admin assistant for a small architectural firm. Her husband was in dental school. They'd furnished their apartment with whatever they could lay their hands on in flea markets and garage sales, but as much as possible they'd followed a black-and-white colour scheme. Now she has decorated her home in soft blues and creams with a little red, in a style the decorators call French Country. She likes its harmony, but misses the promise of that black-and-white apartment. How simple and clear the future seemed then—work and love and art. Her photographs, the collages she built from corrugated cardboard, yogurt cups, Popsicle sticks and matchboxes, all painted white. She hasn't finished an art project in years, except for the decoration of her house, if you can call that art.

DAY FIVE. "BLUE ROOM"

The blue room is white, but Yoko's small, neat handwriting asks her to imagine that it is blue. A television set shows a live video of the sky. Today the sky is a bright cobalt, seeming to lend its blueness to the room. In front of the television, a sign reads, "This is not here." Ann is willing to believe in the absence of the TV set, just as she is willing to believe that "This room gets as wide as an ocean at the other end," and that "This room glows in the dark while we are asleep." Turning around to the ocean-wide end, she reads, "This room gets very narrow like a point at the other end." She feels dizzy and amorphous as if she has plunged briefly into Wonderland, growing within minutes both very large and very small.

She'd like to bring her daughter's fiancé here, to see him in this room. Last night he and Vanessa came for dinner, revealing a diamond and platinum engagement ring. Ann threw her arms around them, wondering—Is this what she wants? He seemed so slight and limited, with his talk of the usefulness of his MBA, with his flyaway brown hair, and the worried frown his face assumed when he wasn't smiling at Vanessa's jokes or holding forth on investment strategies. Ann had wanted the world for her daughter, something big, colourful, and full of surprises, not a shadowy, boxed-in life, an apartment where everything is sawn in half. But perhaps he is as wide as the ocean at one end, while she has only seen the end that is as small as a point.

DAY SIX. "POINTEDNESS"

The point is a glass sphere. On the stand sit Yoko's words: "This sphere will be a sharp point when it gets to the far corners of the room in your mind." If Ann looks at it long enough, perhaps its roundness will fall away to expose the point at its very centre, the core from which it has evolved. Is the essence of the ball its point, its pointy-ness, its antithesis? She imagines the sphere stretching out into the corners of her mind, into its passages and dead ends, transfixing them.

DAY SEVEN. "AMAZE"

Ann drives to the art gallery, cheered by sunshine, daffodils, and forsythia. Maybe Yoko will call today. She spies an empty parking spot, but is distracted by a swirl of orange on the sidewalk, a woman's dress celebrating the warm April day. She expects the traffic to keep flowing in front of her, but it stops abruptly, causing her van to strike a white BMW. She feels like she has collided with something that is not there, or shouldn't have been there. "This is not happening," she says out loud. Now she will have to postpone her visit to the gallery, take her car to the accident reporting station, and maybe tomorrow the body shop. She'll have to calm her husband, who hates for anything to go wrong, and defend her own carelessness, as well as all the time she has been spending at the art gallery. Her thoughts retreat into a familiar cul-de-sac where she often gets stuck, worrying that she has let someone down. Contrite, she doesn't notice how kind the man in the BMW is being.

"Don't worry about it," he says. "It's just the bumper. That's what they're for."

"Are you okay?" she asks.

"I'm in great shape." He flexes his biceps under his shiny suit. He has silver hair and eyes like glossy pebbles in a stream. Ann's husband is growing not silver, but grey and rough like a tree trunk. The silvery man is smooth and sweet as milk. He looks at her bumper.

"Do you want my information?" he asks. "Are you worried?"

"No," she says. The van is seven years old. They have talked about buying her a new car.

"Don't worry," he says. "We'll pretend this never happened."

"This never happened," Ann repeats, feeling it become true. She can hardly see the scratches on her bumper. What looked like a dent reveals itself to be a shadow cast by the sun and the parking sign. "Thank you," she says.

Later, Ann enters the big central room of the exhibit. Just past the phone and the half room stands the maze. Usually a dozen teenagers are lined up, waiting to enter, but today all three rooms are surprisingly quiet. When she slips off her loafers, the white-haired custodian, whose job it is to make sure that only one person enters at a time, waves her in. The walls of the maze are clear plastic, but even though she can see out and people can see in, she has a sense of privacy, of a private, somewhat silly quest, a child's serious game. She walks along, taking the turns, feeling ahead with her hands so that she doesn't bump into any transparent walls. Finding herself in a dead end, she backs up and tries another way. Soon she is in the centre where a white toilet sits, its wooden seat cover down. She could settle here like Rodin's thinker and ponder life. Instead, like everyone else she's watched through the invisible walls, she lifts the cover to look inside at the familiar empty bowl. When Vanessa was four, she used to sit on the toilet making up jokes while she pooped, laughing at her own brilliance, her ability to create two things at once. Ann hadn't thought the jokes were funny, but they'd delighted her clear-eyed daughter who now wants to marry the financial advisor with the flyaway hair.

After she exits the maze and starts to slip her shoes back on, the phone rings. She looks at the custodian, who shrugs, saying, "She hasn't called in a few days."

"I talked to her last week." Ann hurries to answer the phone. Her fingers tremble as she lifts the receiver and hugs it to her ear.

"Who is this?" a woman's voice asks.

It isn't Yoko. Ann doesn't know what to say. "I'm just a visitor to the exhibit."

"Someone there called this number."

"Well, it wasn't me." She hangs up.

"Was it her?" the custodian asks.

"No." Ann drops her hands.

"Sometimes she gets her friends to call, and create situations."

DAY EIGHT. "MOUND OF SORROW. MOUND OF JOY."

Ann returns to the same room the following day. Across from the telephone hang the framed scraps of paper she looked at after Yoko's call. Yoko gave nine of them to a gallery, but there are only six in this show. One is marked with crayon. Was that a child's mischief or intentional—Yoko saying that art is not sacred, but open to other people's additions? Ann found crayon marks on the wall in Duncan's closet when she cleaned his room after he left for university. Angry red and yellow slashes, faded records of some childish tantrum. They must have gestured silently there for at least ten or twelve years, hidden behind games and boxes. Yoko's framed pages are torn, words missing. They are more instructional "paintings," but Ann is tired of reading Yoko's instructions.

She wanders to the other side of the big room where three piles of small grey stones lie on the floor in front of a television showing Yoko and John in bed for peace. The large pile is unnamed, but the other two are marked, "mound of sorrow," and "mound of joy." A woman in a red sweater crouches beside one of the piles, building a stack of stones, each smaller than the last, like the tower of coloured plastic rings Vanessa and Duncan used to play with. Ann had always loved to gather the rings back, in order of size, onto their yellow pole, the colours arranged like a rainbow, while her children slept and she bustled from room to room, tidying traces of the day's activities, attempting to compose the disarray in her own mind and heart.

The joy and sorrow piles seem of equal size, although the stones are arranged differently in each, forming random patterns. Some stones have strayed over the lines that circumscribe joy and sorrow, into the neutral territory between. The woman's tower wobbles a little, but she rests a finger on top, kneeling there as if saying a prayer over her measure of joy.

The voices from the TV sound hollow and ghostly. Ann picks up a stone, rubs it between her fingers, lets it fall with a click onto the mound of sorrow. She has spent half her life erasing the evidence of her children's tantrums and messes, mistakes and disappointments, willing their lives to be perfect and happy, but her power to make them so, always limited, is now lost. Her daughter will marry the small-as-a-point financial advisor. They will lavish their days on jobs in office buildings fifty stories high, and their evenings on each other in an uptown apartment, from which their wastefully lit offices will be visible all night. Her son will become the dentist his father wants him to be, not the singer he could be. He will hum melodies to himself while drilling his patients' teeth. And he will be sad and angry a thousand times over without ever again resolving his feelings into red and yellow strokes made for her to discover.

In the third and final room, across from the wall of doodles, Ann finds the "point" in its 1980s incarnation, not a glass sphere as Yoko conceived it in the sixties, but cast in bronze like the baby shoes Ann keeps locked in a drawer, evidence that her children were once so small they needed her to hold their hands whenever they walked out into the world.

DAY NINE. "FLY"

Ann watches the video in a dark, narrow room, sitting on one of two black leather benches. Is that Yoko's young body the fly leaps and buzzes along, her curves forming a desert landscape for the insect to explore? The soundtrack—Yoko wailing and crooning, playing with sound like a child unaware she is being listened to—reflects either the fly's triumphs and disappointments or the woman's agony at being nothing but the fly's motionless terrain. Ann laughs in delight and horror, delighted at the correlation of Yoko's frantic noises and the fly's apparently aimless quest, horrified as she imagines how it would feel to let a fly probe her lips, tickle her nose, and creep along her naked skin.

She becomes aware that people have entered the room behind her, making the air feel warm and thick. The fly wanders through Yoko's pubic hair. A man sits down on the bench beside Ann. The camera pans back from Yoko, showing her whole body speckled with flies. Ann jumps up and pushes her way out of the room.

The fly had twenty-five minutes on Yoko's body. Ann has had nine days inside her mind. She has completed her mission, but what has she accomplished? Coming here every day was like picking up her children from school—a daily ritual, nothing more or less than that, something to lean on for a time, to build her life around.

She hurries past the maze and the silent telephone, back to the first room where the white walls still pretend to be blue. She stops to look at the broken mornings in their case. If only she'd paid attention to the details of those mornings, she could remember whether the sky had been yellow, silver, or pink, how the light slanted through the window, where it fell on her daughter's cheek or her son's rough hair. If one of these bits of glass could hold all that, she would smash the case for it. She has a few colour photos which capture a mood from back then, some jerky home videos, but that's not what she's missing. If she'd allowed herself to make art all those years—portraits, landscapes, real photographs—she might have noticed more, slowed time with her attention, ceased to wish away the years yearning for her old freedom in the black-and-white apartment. Then maybe now she wouldn't feel so incomplete.

She turns to stare at the box with its shiny glass keys. They blur and warp behind her tears. Yoko told her to take one, but the Plexiglas looks impenetrable. She would have to lift the whole thing from the wall, and carry it out in full view of the guards and visitors. She swipes a tissue across her eyelids, crumples it. Lets it fall. Will someone wonder if it's part of the exhibit, construct meaning from its placement on the floor, conjure up a whole, solid, and convincing portrait of her, the absent agent of its disposal?

Before leaving, she notices a new apple perched on the column. The light forms a splash of white along the green curve of the fruit. Its stem rises to a point. Ann has read that the museum bought a case of organic Granny Smiths from which they replace the bitten and shrivelled ones. She imagines the museum's shadowy basement full of crates overflowing with bright round fruit. Without worrying what anyone might say, she reaches for the apple, and slips it into her purse.

A Large Dark

THREE AND A HALF MONTHS AFTER HIS WIFE LEFT HIM, André had signed up for an evening watercolour class held in a Sunday school classroom at a suburban church. He'd been looking for a way to get out of the house one night a week, to talk to someone other than his son, the nanny, the people at work, to meet a woman who'd praise his paintings and let him take her out to dinner.

One mild Thursday evening in November, a fluorescent ceiling fixture was flickering in the art room. Barry, the white-haired art teacher, lumbered onto a stepstool to try to deactivate it, while André, thirty years younger and at least thirty pounds lighter, pulled a muscle craning his neck and offering unhelpful advice. When Barry finally gave up to let him try, André balanced on the stool, searching for the place where the narrow bulb was attached, but bulb and fixture seemed to be all one, conjoined and wired to the ceiling. Tapping the bulb, he leaned over too far, almost falling onto Barry.

"Don't hurt yourself," Barry said, stone-faced.

André took one last look before jumping down. Massaging his neck, he asked, "Why do they make them like that?"

"To torment us." Barry grinned.

From the portraits on one wall, past ministers, their faces grey and bespectacled, peered out over rows of collapsible tables and plastic chairs, while the windows of the opposite wall reflected the lit figures of the students within.

André returned to his seat, feeling foolish and clumsy. He

was sitting directly across from the flickering light, which promised to give him a headache. He removed his glasses, rubbing the grooves between nose and eyes, then placed the heavy, black-framed lenses onto the table in front of him. He considered moving to a free spot across the room, but Katya, who hadn't arrived yet, always sat beside him, and he liked watching her chestnut hair fall across her face as she leaned in closer to her painting. Katya's missing his attempt at fixing the light had been a lucky break.

Even without his glasses, André could see the reflection of the teacher's paper in the mirror overhanging the table at the front of the room. Barry always tilted the mirror so his students, tired after working all day, could opt to watch him paint from their seats. Consulting his reference, a photo of a seascape, Barry began his demonstration by floating cobalt blue into an orange wash. André relaxed his eyes, tried to breathe deeply. Tonight he hoped to let go of his perfectionism, and allow the paint to flow onto the paper, resisting his tendency to overwork the watercolours until they made thick pasty mud in the shapes of trees. That had been last week's production.

"Do a sketch first to get the composition," Barry was telling the class. "Play with placement. Leave things out. Put them in. Multiply, subtract. It's like math."

"I used to be good at math," André joked. But no one laughed or even turned to look at him.

When Katya appeared in a red jacket, bringing with her the mingled scents of her spicy perfume and the warm night, André thought how he needed a woman to make his life add up again.

"How much have I missed?" she whispered, unpacking her paints.

"Not much." He fiddled with his glasses. He could never think of the right words.

"I used to live by the sea," she said, peering at the reflection of Barry's painting. There was a hint of the Ukraine in her accent.

"My father's family came from Kiev," he said.

"Shh!" said Miriam, the grey-haired woman who sat in front of André.

Katya's eyes were black with flecks of white where the light struck them. "Do you speak Ukrainian?" she whispered.

"No," he said too loudly, causing Miriam and her neighbour to glare at him, but he only noticed Katya's gaze, which flickered like the unfixable light before returning to Barry's painting in the mirror.

André put on his glasses to watch Barry write in the details with a long narrow brush, a form of calligraphy, shaping fine, finger-like branches and a flourish of leaves.

"A few more touches," Barry said. "And it's done."

"You said I didn't miss anything." Katya frowned.

"I didn't want to upset you," he said. But she'd already grabbed her sketchbook and was dashing to the front of the room to join the students crowded around Barry's table.

André followed. He wanted to say something that would make her smile in gratitude, or even admiration. He watched her study Barry's painting and scribble in her book.

Up close, the painting looked sketchy and insubstantial. When André took a few steps back, it started to gain strength. Its power lay not in its strokes and colours, but in the way they played off each other, the contrast of light and dark, the illusion they created of moodiness and movement. The rocks and branches in the foreground seemed to beckon to the glistening sailboat on the horizon where the deep indigo of the ocean faded into mauve.

"I don't know how you do it," he said to Barry.

"Practice," Barry said. "That's all it takes."

André didn't believe him. He suspected there was some trick Barry was keeping to himself, that to make the magic work he'd need to find the right brand and shades of paint, the right weight and grain of paper, the exact alchemical formula.

"Is that a new red?" he asked, leaning over the table to point to a deep crimson next to the yellows on Barry's palette. Some of the other students moved in to examine the colour.

"No," Barry said. "That's just alizarin."

"I thought so," said Miriam, who'd left her seat to take a closer look. She shook her head at André. "You're always suspecting a colour conspiracy."

He shrugged. "It looked different tonight."

Barry scraped the edge of a razor blade across the paper to make flecks of white surf. "I'm going to stop there," he said.

"Beautiful," Katya said.

The students dispersed. André followed Katya back to her seat. He watched her tape paper to a board and squeeze paint onto her palette.

"Is this sable?" He picked up one of her brushes, stroking it across the knuckles of his other hand, imagining Katya's lush brown hair falling against his skin.

"Just start your painting." She pushed him away. "Get on with it. You're up to your old delaying tactics. You have to jump in, get your brush wet."

"So to speak." He smiled. "You won't let me get away with anything." The place on his shoulder where she'd touched him felt warm. His shirtsleeve, resting lightly against his skin, seemed to kiss the imprint of her hand. Maybe it would be a good night after all.

He looked at his copy of the photo Barry had given the class. It differed a little from the teacher's. The boat was larger, closer to the shore, and there was an island. He made a small sketch to get the composition right. Then he laid down washes, lost himself in the act of painting. He looked up when Barry walked by, nodding at him. That meant things were going okay, so far. He painted the oblong of a big rock, but started to do the shadow too soon, and the paint ran. That flower of dark spreading across the rock tweaked his old impatience with himself. He felt the bad mood rise in his chest, rush through his blood. Now he wouldn't be able to finish. Now the night was goddamn ruined. Liz was the one responsible for these moods. The goddamn divorce couldn't come soon enough. Katya was painting happily beside him, her rock edged and shadowed in three bold, innocent strokes.

He tried to fix his painting, adding more rocks to conceal the blurry shadow, using a palette knife to scrape away some of the paint and create planes of light where the sun hit the foreground. But when he stepped back, he saw that the rocks were too big and too much alike, and the white sailboat, which was supposed to be sailing bravely out of the harbour, seemed to be drawn hopelessly towards them.

"I've had enough," he said.

"Leaving early again?" Miriam asked.

André packed up his paints and brushes. "I'll finish it at home," he said, knowing he wouldn't. "My son's waiting for me."

Intent on her painting, Katya didn't respond, didn't even look his way.

"I'm done," he said as he passed Barry at the front of the room.

One side of Barry's mouth turned up, more a grimace than a smile. "You should try to stay for the critique sometime. You might learn something."

André shrugged, and adjusted the shoulder strap of his black portfolio. "I have to get home to my son before bedtime."

Barry turned away. André stood there waiting for some-thing—another word from his teacher, absolution, praise for being a good father, a wave from Katya, a nod from Miriam. But heads were lowered, intent on finishing touches, and Barry stood silent, immovable, arms crossed, ready for the students to bring him their paintings so he could place them one at a time on the easel for critique.

André hurried out the door to the parking lot. Pulling his keys from his pocket, searching for the right one, he dropped them onto the pavement. "Goddamn!" He leaned his portfolio against the black Jeep, and bent down to retrieve the keys. The November night smelled fresh as spring, but, flushed with anger and hot in his leather jacket, he couldn't enjoy it, didn't know when he'd last enjoyed anything. He'd yet to finish a painting, and each week it seemed less and less likely that Katya would go out with him, that he'd even find the words to ask her.

At home, he dropped his portfolio onto the floor next to Braden's running shoes, removed his jacket, and hung it in the closet.

"Daddy!" his son's voice squealed from upstairs. "I'm still awake."

"I'll be up in a minute," André called. He unlaced his work shoes, slipped on leather moccasins, and headed for the kitchen, his footsteps echoing through the big, empty house. He imagined Katya sitting at the kitchen table with a bowl of hot borscht, her lips crimson from the beets. Then, noticing the dirty dishes in the sink, his familiar anger flooded back. He'd planned to make hot chocolate for three—himself, Braden, and Bridget, the nanny. Now Bridget wouldn't get a mug. He filled the kettle, and switched on the burner. She always let him down just when he'd started to hope she was on top of her job. She hadn't even wiped the counters. She'd probably say Braden hadn't left her alone for one minute, that she was hired as nanny not housekeeper. But he'd been very clear about her responsibilities when she'd first arrived. One good thing about Liz—she'd been fanatical about the house, couldn't go to bed at night if the kitchen wasn't clean, or out the door in the morning without vacuuming the wall-to-wall.

He filled the mugs with hot water, stirred in the mix. No, he wasn't in the mood for marshmallows tonight. Braden would be disappointed, but he just couldn't reach into that high cupboard, undo the twist tie on the bag, smell that whiff of vanilla. Damn Liz! Even a marshmallow could remind him of her, how she used to bake for him during what she referred to as her Suzy Homemaker phase, when she'd taken a six-month leave from her job at the art gallery while they'd tried to get pregnant.

He'd loved coming home to a wife fragrant with baking, her cotton pullover dusted with flour, her tongue sweet from cookie dough or cake batter. He remembered licking a smudge of chocolate off her chin as he undressed her on the living-room rug. When they'd failed to conceive, she'd claimed that his enthusiasm for getting her pregnant was making her feel ambivalent, afraid of becoming what he seemed so much to want her to be—nothing more or less than a mother and a wife.

"I don't feel like myself," she'd said. "I need to go back to work so I can remember why having a baby seemed like a good idea."

"Fine," he'd said. "But no more ten-hour days or skipping lunch. Your body is going to be nourishing our child."

When she'd finally gotten pregnant, he'd tried to persuade her to quit work for good, to leave those modern monstrosities of paint and plaster behind to stay home with the baby.

"You can start painting again in your spare time," he'd said.

"What spare time? At least at the gallery I can talk about painting, and help other artists get their work noticed."

Liz had taken the standard maternity leave, and André had spent two weeks at home, sleeping in with her, cooking big breakfasts while she nursed Braden, the three of them napping on their queen-size bed through the quiet winter afternoons. If he woke before Braden, he'd bury his face between Liz's heavy breasts, counting the seconds to discover how long he could hold his breath, then tasting each nipple to see which one was sweeter.

"The left one today." He'd held it between his fingers, watching the milk spurt up in a thin bluish fountain.

"Bradie doesn't notice any difference," Liz had said, turning away to stroke their son's sleeping face. "You always have to be judging everything."

Even with Liz's moodiness, those two weeks stood out as the happiest of his life, but, returning to the law firm, he'd been penalized for them, his biggest client handed over to one of the junior partners.

Holding the hot mugs out in front of him, André walked upstairs, watching for toys on the steps.

Braden was in bed, reading his favourite book—*Green Eggs and Ham*. His fine brown hair had been cut short and straight across his forehead by André's barber. The soft down on his cheeks and nose glowed in the lamplight, which cast his shadow, large and diffuse, onto the opposite wall.

"Daddy!" He put down his book. "Hot chocolate!"

André set Braden's mug onto the bedside table. "Where's Bridget?"

"In her room. She got a phone call."

Long distance no doubt. Better not be collect. Bridget had dozens of long-winded friends and relatives in New Brunswick, where she'd grown up and lived until just a few months ago.

"No marshmallows?" Braden asked, showing André his sad face, lower lip pushed out, hound dog eyes.

"Not tonight. How was school?"

"We made poppies for Remember Day, to remember the soldiers who died. Mrs. Skinner put my poppy on the wall."

"Good." André sipped his cocoa, thinking of his high school art teacher, Mrs. Flynn, how she'd praised him, misleading him to believe he could be an artist. Now, with Barry's terse encouragement, he was trying to paint again. Liz would laugh at him if she found out. She used to call watercolours old-lady paintings.

"What about Winslow Homer?" he'd asked her. "What about Sargent? Their watercolours are more artful than those blobs of paint on a canvas you love so much."

"They were both old ladies," she'd replied with that tenderly mocking smile of hers.

Would she call him an old lady too? Would she call Katya

an old lady? Katya's paintings made Barry's eyes light up. Liz did used to say that André was old-fashioned. When they were dating, she had seemed to like that about him, liked how he'd worn a tie when he took her out to dinner, and opened the car door for her. But sometime during their marriage, it had become a deficit, a sticking point.

Braden said, "We're singing a song for Remember Day in the gym. Can you and Mommy come watch me?"

"Sorry, Bradie, I have to work."

"Can you ask Mommy?"

"I guess so." A brief spasm shot through his chest, a mere twinge of what he'd feel if he phoned Liz. Even if he called her, she might not show up, too busy with her new job in acquisitions, paying ridiculous sums of money for paintings that looked like nothing at all. There'd been a picture of one in the paper yesterday—a plain blue canvas with a snaking yellow line. The brashness of it had made his eyes itch. Katya's paintings had an abstract quality, but they always suggested something real.

He grabbed hold of Braden's hand, gently squeezing it. "I wish I could be there to hear your class sing."

"That's okay. Mommy will come."

"She may be busy." She didn't see enough of Braden, but the little she did was too much for André. He begrudged her any part of the comforting burden of their son's love.

"Goodnight." He kissed Braden's forehead, and turned off the light.

With the dark came panic like a rush of water into his lungs. He had to breathe slowly and deeply to make it recede. To-morrow he'd talk to Liz. Right now he wanted to fall into bed and forget. He heard the kettle hiss. Bridget was off the phone, making herself a hot drink. He'd tell her she had to smarten up if she wanted to stay. But when he entered the kitchen, she was washing the dishes.

"Do you want some tea?" she asked, her face flushed and

smiling, as if she'd been on the phone with a boyfriend.

"No thanks. Braden and I had hot chocolate."

Even the back of her neck where it met her shoulders was pink. He remembered kissing Liz in that exact spot while she stood stirring cake batter. He'd felt her muscles move under his lips as she leaned back against him.

Bridget was wearing a T-shirt and flannel pyjama pants. He wanted to stand close behind her, to lift the T-shirt off over her head. But she was nineteen, exactly half his age, and Braden's nanny. He felt nauseous with fatigue and confusion. If only he'd worked up the nerve to ask Katya out.

"Goodnight." He headed for the stairs, rubbing his neck.

André didn't mind the morning drive. He listened to the all-news channel, and reviewed his schedule for the day. But his drive home that night killed him. As his Jeep crawled along the highway, his bones aching, he kicked the day around in his head. There'd been a client's complaints, a hint from the senior partner that he wasn't clocking enough hours, a co-worker's snide remark about his choice of tie: "Wife pick that one out for you, Andy?" Had that been deliberate cruelty? Did the man realize that André no longer had a wife?

"You hate it there," Liz would have told him. "When are you going to start your own practice like you're always saying?" He'd put off phoning her all day. He'd have to call tonight. After dinner. He hoped Bridget had remembered to cook the fresh salmon he'd bought at the market.

When he opened the door, Bridget was sprawled across the sofa, reading a novel, while Braden sat inches from the blaring television. He wondered what Katya was doing right now, tried to picture her relaxing after work in soft, old jeans like the ones Liz used to wear, but he couldn't envision her surroundings, and realized he knew nothing about her life outside of class.

"Turn that thing down," he yelled.

Bridget reached for the remote.

"What have you done about dinner?" He removed his glasses, rubbing his eyes.

"It's fish sticks and French fries," Bridget said without looking at him. "Yours is in the oven. Braden and I have already eaten."

"What happened to the salmon I brought home yesterday?"

"I'll make it tomorrow."

"It won't be fresh tomorrow. That fish cost me twenty bucks."

"D'you want me to cook it now?" She stood up, hands on hips.

"You can do it in the microwave with teriyaki sauce. It'll take five minutes."

"So why don't you make it yourself?"

"Why don't I do everything myself? Because I pay you to help me do the things I don't have the time or energy for."

"Well, I want a raise." She glared at him, challenging him like a teenage girl standing up to her father. With her clear, blue-grey eyes, pink and white skin, and the freckles scattered across her nose, she could have been Braden's sister. "If you want me to do all this fancy cooking, I want a raise."

"We'll talk about it later," he said, suddenly exhausted. "Just cook the salmon and make a salad while I change."

Bridget stomped into the kitchen.

Braden continued watching television. André wondered how many times his son had had to do this very thing—enter that other reality in order to tune out his parents' fighting. He wished he could crawl in there with him. Often he too sought refuge in television, the Internet, or one of the other distractions life offered with such apparent generosity—work, drink, anger. Painting was different. He'd followed it like any other escape route away from himself, from the memory of Liz saying that all he was to her was a big mistake, but every week it led him right back to that cracked place inside.

When André came downstairs, Bridget was fixing a salad. "Since I'm making salad for you, I might as well make some for myself. I need to eat more healthy. You've got so much junk food around here."

"You don't have to eat the junk food. The chips and cookies are treats for Braden, not for you to stuff your face all day."

She slit her eyes at him.

"You should be more respectful. If I was this rude to my boss, she'd fire me in a second."

"So why don't you fire me?" She tilted her head, and a hint of a smile crossed her face, as if she guessed why, as if she wasn't really angry.

"If you don't smarten up..." He couldn't finish his sentence. He didn't want to fire Bridget. He wanted to kiss her.

"I do my job," she said. "Braden likes me. I take good care of him. I don't see why I have to uphold your bourgeois standards and fancy foods."

"Because that's what I pay you to do." His skin tingled with something like happiness. "I pay you to uphold my bourgeois standards, and take care of my bourgeois child." Arguing with Bridget felt fun and bracing like a game, not like fights with Liz, which had left him feeling damaged and desolate. "And I pay you to help me create a comfortable, nurturing environment for him so that his mother doesn't have a leg to stand on if she tries to get custody."

"Will she try?" Bridget looked down at the rings of red pepper she'd just sliced on the cutting board, her splendid anger dissolved into sympathy.

He shouldn't have mentioned Liz, or even thought about her. "She doesn't seem to know what she wants."

"She hardly ever comes to see him." Bridget dumped the pepper rings into the salad. "It looks like you're safe."

"It's not safety I want."

The next day, he came home to a clean house and a pot of homemade chili.

"Have you thought about that raise?" Bridget asked, while the three sat eating.

"This is good." Braden smiled conspiratorially at Bridget.

"Thanks. It's my father's recipe."

"Okay," André said, "but you have to keep this up."

"Keep what up?" she asked, wide-eyed.

"You know what. The cleaning and cooking, the stuff you're paid to do."

"Whatever." The kitchen light seemed to shine right through her skin, making it as translucent as one of Barry's washes.

André watched the corners of her eyes and mouth turn up into a private, self-congratulatory smile, the kind of smile he'd sometimes caught on Liz's face in the middle of breakfast, or when she kicked off her heels after coming home late from work. He'd never seen Katya smile like that. She grinned openly or not at all.

"Is Mommy coming to my assembly?" Braden asked.

"I'm going to call her tonight."

The last time they'd spoken, he'd found himself yelling into the phone. She'd picked up Braden from school without telling André first.

"This yelling is the reason I didn't call you," she'd said. "I'd like to see Braden more often, but I hate having to go through you all the time."

"You should have thought of that before you left."

"You know this isn't working, André."

"Braden and I are fine."

"He needs his mother."

"You think we can't function without you, that we spend our time moping around the house, but you're wrong. We're both fine. So why don't you just leave us alone."

"My lawyer is going to call," she'd warned. But so far, he hadn't heard.

Thursday, Katya was early. She set her paints beside André's.

"I didn't want to miss the demo."

"It's a still life."

She wrinkled her nose. "I prefer a good landscape."

"Still life's okay. Maybe I can get it right this time."

"It's not about right. When are you going to learn that?"

"It's all about getting it right," he said. "Sometimes the gods smile but most of the time they don't."

Miriam turned in her chair to look at him. "You have it all wrong," she said. "The gods can't smile unless you do."

André frowned. He suspected the women of mocking him.

"You don't smile much, do you?" Katya laughed.

He resolved to work up a smile for her.

Barry was composing the still life—one half of a watermelon lay on its cut side like a dark green hill, the other, sliced into wedges, revealed its red flesh and black seeds. He placed one wedge in front of the melon hill and one behind, then added a spray of purple leaves to partially conceal the bulk of the fruit.

"Okay," he said. "I'm going to start with a sketch." He roughed in the melon pieces and the leaves with a soft pencil. "I like that composition. It makes a nice negative shape of the background. I'm going to have a small dark—the leaves and the dark stripes on the melon rind." He shaded them heavily. "A large mid-tone—the melons and the cast shadow. And a medium-sized light—the background and the reflections on the fruit. You might choose to make the background larger and have a medium-sized mid-tone, but this is the way I'm doing it."

André thought he'd do it that way too. He'd yet to see one of Barry's paintings go awry. He watched in the overhanging mirror while Barry put paint to paper, and, without any apparent thought or effort, conjured bright images.

Eager to begin, he followed Barry's lead, and let his painting take shape under his brush, exploring the curve of the melon rind and the vibrancy of its flesh where crimson blended into rose madder. He remembered to leave triangles and squares of white paper for the highlights. He forgot about himself, forgot about Katya sitting beside him, the other students bent over their paintings, and Barry making his rounds, until the teacher stood behind him.

"Leave it there," Barry said. "You've got it. If you keep painting you're going to muddy it."

André set down his brush. "Do you think it's done?"

"It's very nice. Especially that melon wedge in the foreground. You've captured the different tones there very nicely. I like this soft pink background and the feathery quality of the leaves against the strong melon shapes. Everything works to set off that red flesh."

"That's a good painting," Katya said.

"Beautiful," said Miriam.

André felt his chest swell, as when strangers admired his son. "Finally, I got it."

"You got it once," Barry said. "That'll be enough to keep you going until the next time. Why don't you start another while you're on a roll? And try staying for critique tonight."

André prepared another piece of paper, taping the edges to the board. He sketched the composition on a drawing pad. This time he'd make a large dark—a close-up focusing on the big curve and dark stripes of the melon's skin. But when he picked up his brush, the blank paper made him think about his marriage, and caused his hand to tremble.

One night, a few weeks before she'd left, Liz had said, "I've never felt loved by you."

"I tell you I love you all the time." He'd stared at her pale lashes, the whites of her eyes.

"You're always either finding fault with the things that are important to me—the paintings I admire, the installations and artists at work—or putting me on a pedestal, like I'm this domestic goddess that I'm just so tired of trying to be."

"That's not how it is. You're the one always finding fault with me. You never say it outright, but you think I'm a failure, that I don't have the guts to start my own practice. *You* don't love *me*."

"That's not true."

But she'd proven him right. All that stuff about not feeling loved had just been an excuse.

Even now his chest felt heavy with the memory of her lying to him. Starting to wheeze and cough, he fled to the adjacent kitchen for a drink.

Katya sauntered in to freshen her painting water. "You look flushed. Are you sick?" she asked.

"It's hot in here." Everything looked blurred, undefined. He searched for his glasses in his empty shirt pocket.

"I'm a nurse, you know." She peered into his eyes. "I see sick people all day. Are you sure you're not sick?"

"Maybe I am." He'd heard her tell Miriam that she was a nurse, but he'd forgotten. Nursing had seemed too prosaic a career for Katya. Now she was leaning so close to him that he was able to see her clearly without his glasses—her velvety hair, her skin reddish beneath high cheekbones, the smile lines on either side of her mouth. He kept still, enjoying her nearness, feeling his breath quicken.

"Maybe I have a serious illness that requires lots of nursing."

"No," she said, slowly sizing him up. "You look all right to me. I'm more worried about my melon. It doesn't look well at all."

"Oh." He rubbed his neck, still sore from last week's attempt at fixing the light, which had since been dismantled, so that tonight only the shell of the fixture remained.

When Katya looked at him, did she see what Liz saw? What Bridget saw? Lately Bridget had been moping around the house. Last night he'd scolded her for serving half-cooked fish sticks and leaving the laundry in the dryer to wrinkle. She'd burst into tears, and wept openly on the sofa, making him feel like a brute.

"I'm sorry," he'd repeated half a dozen times, kneeling in front of her with a box of Kleenex.

She'd laughed then, reaching out a hand as if to caress his face, but only touching one finger to the tip of his nose.

He decided to try one more time with Katya. "Show me your painting," he said. The swirling strokes of red and orange made the melons look wild, but still recognizable, unlike the fruits and flowers Liz used to paint before they were married, her large canvases laden with impenetrable slabs of colour.

"Very nice. You just need some highlights and a cast shadow here."

"Of course. I forgot the shadow. Thanks." She turned her back on him, and filled her brush with paint.

He contemplated the sketch he'd prepared. It was okay, but there wasn't enough time for him to start a new watercolour. Instead he walked around the room and looked at everyone else's. Returning to his seat, viewing his painting from a distance, his face grew hot. It was fucking amateurish. His colours weren't as clear as he'd thought. The purple splotch on the melon's flesh, which had seemed a charming rendition of a bruise, now looked like a mistake.

Next to his painting lay the blank paper. He'd thought it had reminded him of his marriage because that's how they'd started—with a fresh sheet on which they'd both proceeded to hurl paint and make a mess. But maybe Liz was the white paper, not blank, but exposed to a constant source of light that cast a blinding reflection. Is that why she'd stopped painting? Had his opinions discouraged her? He remembered now that the six months she'd taken off work had been meant as a sabbatical, a time for her to paint. But Liz had felt blocked.

"I can't work here," she'd said, furiously whisking egg whites for a soufflé. "I get distracted by housework and cooking. And the lighting is too harsh."

"Those are just excuses," he'd said. "If you really wanted to paint, none of that would matter."

"If I really wanted to paint, I'd find a more supportive part-ner," Liz had yelled, flinging the foamy egg at André's face.

He'd thought their marriage was perfect, but maybe she'd been telling the truth about never feeling loved. Maybe disappointment was what had made her restless and bitter, disappointment in the meagerness of his love. So stingy he couldn't even give his own son a marshmallow or make the phone call Braden had trusted him to make, inviting Liz to hear him sing at school. Or summon the courage to turn off the light that made the things it shone on appear either brightly perfect or horrifyingly blank.

He sat hunched over his still life, staring at the backs of the other students' heads, until Katya said, "That's your breakthrough painting. You're getting the hang."

"I don't like it. The fruit's too dark."

"It's stormy. I know I complain about still life, but it's really the same as landscape, only on a smaller scale. You've got another seascape there. That melon's a ship."

"Then how do you explain all that pink?"

"That's dawn." Katya grinned.

"Don't say, it's darkest before the dawn," André groaned.

"You rescued mine. See how the shadows ground the fruit? They looked like they were floating before."

"Let's go out for coffee to celebrate." He blurted the words before remembering how she'd rejected him in the kitchen.

"I'm meeting someone after." She flipped back the hair on one side of her face, as if tossing André back into a pond.

"Me too." He gulped for the breath he'd missed while awaiting her answer. "I forgot I have a date with my son for hot chocolate." He hastily packed his brushes and paints before Barry could catch him for critique.

At home, a strange red car blocked the driveway. Liz's new car. André's hands tightened around the steering wheel as he parked on the street.

The house was dark. He switched on a light, listened for Braden's voice. Nothing. He strode upstairs, peered into Braden's room. The bed was empty. Liz had taken his son. André felt his heart plummet, as if the cracks in his chest had finally given way, and sent everything crashing. But why was her car still here? They must be somewhere in the house. Why hadn't he thought to seek out Bridget in the basement? He knew he'd find them there—Bridget and Liz—all chummy, chatting like women do, no secrets, their men revealed, exposed. He sprinted downstairs, but stalled halfway, hearing a muffled voice. Heart beating fast, he found himself calling her name, a hopeful, soft "Liz," surfacing from his chest. But when he got to the bottom of the stairs, all he saw through the open door was Bridget on the phone.

"I'll call you back, Mum," she said.

"Where are they?"

"She took him down the street to a friend's. They should be back any minute. I told her you'd be home soon."

"She could've taken him away," he said, his voice breaking. "You shouldn't even let her into the house!"

"But she's his mother."

He took off his glasses, wiped his sleeve across his forehead. "You shouldn't have answered the door."

"Now I'll know." She spoke softly, careful of him. She sounded older, nearly maternal. Liz hadn't spoken kindly to him in so long.

"It's okay," Bridget said, as he slid his arms around her, letting his forehead rest against hers.

She seemed to be pardoning his mistakes, erasing his failures, easing his guilt.

"I'm leaving in a couple weeks." She pulled away, her face as pink as it had been a week ago when he'd thought she'd been on the phone with a boyfriend.

"Am I that hard to work for?"

"It's nothing to do with you. I miss home too much."

He leaned towards her again. She let him kiss her.

He felt a space open in his chest. "Whatever you want to do is fine," he said. He wanted to do something large and generous for her, send her home tomorrow with three month's wages.

The thought made him feel almost happy. But then he'd have to find someone else to look after his son.

"You'd better go," Bridget said, her face even pinker, as she pushed him out the door.

"I have to go get Braden," he said.

He hadn't seen Liz and Braden together in months; she'd always arranged her visits to coincide with André's absences.

He stood on the sidewalk, arms crossed in front of his chest, and waited for Liz, unable to think what he might say to her. For now his neck had stopped hurting. It felt easy and warm as he sketched circles with his head. But he could feel the weather changing, a cold wind piecing itself together out of the silky November night.

His eyes grew dry and sore from staring down the street, almost forgetting to blink, until two shadows—one large, one small—emerged from the dark. He squinted as they passed under a street lamp, but the light did nothing to make their pairing less strange, or less natural.

Lemon Curl

WITHIN THE LOW, GREYING BERMUDA LIMESTONE WALL grows a further wall of pink oleander, bordering the lemon grove. A big arching white cedar stands across from the lemon trees. Under its shade, no grass will grow, and the ground, red from the iron-rich soil, lies bare and soft. A curving gravel path leads up past rose bushes and nasturtiums to a small white house with dark green shutters. Twelve years ago, before she and Larry bought the property, Liv had asked the owners if the lemons were edible. She'd understood from childhood that the milky sap of oleanders was poisonous, and wondered if the poison might leach into the soil. The owners had told her not to worry; they'd been eating the lemons for years.

One morning, towards the close of 1982, lemons fall from the tree and tumble through the rain-soaked air. Liv is falling too, although looking at her, you can see no movement of any kind. She lies flat on her stomach in bed, face pressed into the pillow so that you wonder how she can breathe, or if she is alive at all.

If you could see inside Liv's head, you'd be struck by the jumble of brightly coloured images—plump oranges, yellow and red lantana, striped horse jumps, translucent purple jellyfish, small pink hands, achingly white sails—all falling at different speeds, all subject to gravity. At one time, Liv had managed to keep the images circling, holding them in the air like a juggler—talented, promising Liv, who had dreamed of starting a horse-riding school and breeding horses, but who has instead found herself alone with a brood of children and a grove full of lemons.

Her children are stretched out in various positions on the living-room floor, playing Monopoly, travelling past Go, collecting two hundred dollars, going to jail, constantly surprised by their good, bad, and indifferent luck.

"Oh, shit!" says Lucy when she lands on Boardwalk, owned by her brother, Luke, who added a house to his property each time he passed Go.

"Pay up." Luke holds out his palm.

"I'll have to mortgage my railroads and sell my hotels. Shit and damn!" At seven, Lucy loves to practice her swearing in her parents' absence.

"Watch your mouth," warns her older sister, Laina.

"Just because Mom's sick doesn't make you the boss." Lucy dumps her hotels into the cardboard box.

"Mom's not sick," Luke says. "She's gone mental."

"Don't say that!" Lucy hurls her favourite playing piece, a Scottie dog, at her brother's face. The steel clinks against his tooth.

"That hurt, you little shit." Luke jumps for Lucy, grabbing onto her tangled blonde hair.

"Stop it!" Laina rushes to separate them. Play money and plastic houses scatter over the board. "That's enough," she says in exactly their mother's old tone.

"I'm sick of you both." Luke glares at his sisters.

"Go to hell." Laina dumps the Monopoly board back into the box.

The screen door slams behind Lucy as she hurtles across the rose garden in the rain. When she reaches the steps leading down to the grove of trees, she stops to pull up her sagging knee socks. Rain pelts her head and skin. If you listen carefully, you can pick out the tune of the song she sings to make herself feel happy again. It's one of the reggae songs her father used to play on the stereo—Bob Marley's "Three Little Birds." She skips down the steps and climbs the old white cedar. Under its sheltering branches, the rain becomes a drizzle. Years ago, her father nailed a platform up there and called it a tree fort. That was for Luke, but Lucy is the one who uses it most. The nails are rusty now, and the boards shift a little under her weight. "Don't worry," she sings. Through the trailing leaves, she can see her mother's lemon trees, the plump yellow fruit glistening between dark shiny leaves, the fallen lemons like wet grenades in the slick crab grass.

Lucy climbs down for some. They are so ripe their rinds are almost orange. She knows they'll taste as sweet as lemonade, not like the lemons from the grocery store, or the ones served in iced tea at restaurants in town. They never go out to eat anymore. She hasn't had a hamburger or fried chicken in over six months. They eat hot dogs, grilled cheese, canned soup, mostly prepared by Laina. Back in the tree, Lucy digs her fingernails into the thin lemon rind, which pulls easily from the fruit. She lets the curling pieces of rind fall to the earth. Her mother says that these lemons are a superior variety, what all lemons should be like, but Lucy cannot remember the name. She thinks it begins with an M.

Liv has not stirred except for a slight shift in the position of her head to seek air. The movement in and out of her nostrils is soft and slow. She can subsist on very little. Lately she rouses herself only when Laina brings her tea or soup. She'd wanted to name Laina Toby after Larry's dead father, but Larry had said he didn't want to be reminded of the past every time he looked at his daughter. He was the one who chose the children's names, continuing the alliterative trend he and Liv had accidentally begun. She'd thought it silly until he persuaded her that the L's were a way of declaring their unity, of looping them all closer together.

Each time Laina sets cup and saucer onto the nightstand, the sight of her crinkled forehead stirs Liv's guilt. A twelve year old shouldn't have to take care of her mother. Liv tugs at one of the round leather buttons on her wool cardigan, clutches it to her chest, feeling herself slide ever closer to the hard, bare place she senses at the end. Don't they call it rock bottom? Isn't she there yet?

Laina hates weekends. She can't have friends over, and she can't go anywhere without her siblings. Her life has become a box she moves within. On one side are her brother and sister. On the opposite side lies her mother. The third side is school. And the last side, the one that walls her off most completely from herself, is the need she feels to keep people from knowing, to pretend that everything in their house is normal.

Laina returns the Monopoly game to the closet, notices the vacuum cleaner, and decides the house needs a good cleaning. The vacuum sucks up dried grass and mud tracked in from the garden, Cheerios and corn flakes spilled on the carpet, crinkled curls of paper cast off from the children's notebooks. Its loud hum drowns out the silence oozing from Luke's and her mother's rooms. She imagines Luke behind his closed door, lying flat on his stomach across his bed, face lost in his pillow.

Laina wipes the cedar coffee table with a damp cloth, erasing the sticky fingerprints and smears of chocolate her brother and sister have left there. She thinks of what Aunt Carol said when she was visiting from England a few months ago—that Luke would miss his father most because he's a boy, and boys should not have to grow up without their fathers. Laina has always loved Aunt Carol, who has a British accent, wears short skirts, and tells stories about her many boyfriends, but when she said that about Luke, Laina felt her stomach twist. She wanted to scream that it wasn't true. Laina is the one who misses their father most, and hates him most too, because, as everyone always said, she was his favourite, and she will never understand how he could leave her behind.

Liv thinks of the time before the children because those are the years that seem most truly happy. The June day she and Larry first met at a party on the beach, when everyone had returned from their American and Canadian universities. He walked her home, and they kissed on the swing in her parents' garden until the stars came out. A week or two later, she took him for a boat cruise in the lemony sunlight amongst the islands of Hamilton Harbour, then out to Somerset where they docked at Lantana for lunch under pink umbrellas. Larry drank beer from a chilled mug. Liv sipped Planters' Punch, the dark rum floating on top, sweet and strong on her tongue, like the sun that was burning her skin, like Larry stroking her body in a private cove, where they crouched half-submersed in the salty water. He scraped his calf on a limestone reef, and she would never forget the sudden bruising pressure of his fingers on her forearm, his yelp of pain, or the tears that bent his lashes.

Luke removes the screen from his window and climbs through, dropping softly to the ground. He doesn't want Laina to know where he's going. Luke is a boy full of secrets. His biggest secret is that he doesn't really miss his father. It's his mother he misses. She never wanders into his room at night anymore. He used to hear her soft footsteps, feel her hand rest on his forehead, smell her lavender hand lotion as he floated back to sleep. Lately, bereft of her hovering presence, he wakes abruptly from nightmares. Last night he was chasing her wheeled coffin, which rolled ahead of him like an old-fashioned racing car past pink and yellow houses until it was so far ahead that he knew he'd never catch it.

Luke lets himself out the back gate, closes it behind him. Before setting off down the road, he takes a deep breath as if steeling himself for adventure. You can tell that each stride fills him with a sense of freedom and forgetting. The rain has stopped, the clouds are parting, and the asphalt sparkles in the sun. His bare arms feel warm even though it's only two weeks until Christmas. His grandparents will be coming from the States. Maybe they can get his mother out of bed. Luke climbs onto the limestone wall that skirts the road and walks along the top of it, picking petals off hibiscus, doing battle with long flexible oleander stalks, popping acid-green cherry leaves into his mouth. At the end of the road, he jumps off to cross the busy street before following rough stone steps down to the water. Even though winter is near, it's a fine Saturday afternoon, and a few people are boating. A warm breeze ripples across the harbour. Luke breathes in the salty air with its tang of sulphur, feeling his body soften.

His father used to take them out in the motorboat. There it sits, glistening on the water. It's not fair that they don't use it anymore. All alone out there, the boat will rot or sink. Someone needs to watch it, or put it away for the winter. He climbs into the small rowboat, moored at the dock, grabs the oars and rows out to the motorboat. You can easily read its embarrassing name, "Liv and Larn," painted on the stern in bold blue script, and understand why Luke wants to take a stone and scratch out the "Larn." Tying up to the boat's mooring, he pulls on the rope until he is close enough to jump aboard.

Liv remembers the blue ribbons she won jumping horses when she was young, how her horse, Ringo, had responded to the slightest pressure of her knees as he carried her over white gates and stiff green hedges. Ringo's love and loyalty had been exclusive and had lasted until his sudden death while Liv was away at university. She can still make herself cry by reading the letter in which her mother described his heart attack, a letter Liv received on a sunny October morning when she was planning to skip classes for a drive in the country with a tall, shy philosophy student she'd been flirting with for weeks. After spending the afternoon weeping on his shoulder, she refused to see him again because she couldn't look into his dark, attentive eyes without thinking of Ringo.

Luke finds a sponge under a seat. He sops up the rainwater that has collected in the stern, grimacing as he squeezes the sponge dry. He pulls a key from his pocket, another of his secrets. He'd found it in the kitchen drawer reserved for odds and ends, the place his father had always kept it. He tells himself that he only wants to see if the engine is still running, but once he hears its steady growl, he can't resist taking the boat for a spin. That's what his father used to say—"Hey, sport, want to go for a spin?"

Luke pulls in the bumpers, releases the boat from its mooring, and starts off with a burst of speed, which lifts the bow so that he can't see what's ahead. Slowing it a little to reach a plane, he heads towards the islands where they used to anchor for a swim and a picnic. Luke wishes he had one of his mother's tuna sandwiches now, along with a thermos of lemonade, but he forgets about food as the cool air rushes at his face, the salt spray splashes his arms, and the sun warms the top of his head. He has driven the boat plenty of times, but always with his parents and sisters along. Now he feels different—older, freer, more excited, and more afraid. The hairs on his arms and legs rise. His scalp tingles.

Liv's foot twitches as if she would like to kick someone. She's reliving one of the fights she and Larry had before they were married. They'd been snorkelling amongst the coral reefs. Liv's head was still full of the brightly coloured fishes she'd seen—red squirrel fish, blue and yellow angelfish, a milky purple man-o-war, the pale green body of a moray eel whose head was hidden inside the reef. Larry was trying to start the engine, which sputtered as it ran out of gas.

"I asked you if the tank was full," Liv said.

"No, you didn't," Larry argued. "I assumed your father had filled it up after the weekend."

"Why should my father keep the tank full for us?"

"He usually does."

"Not after the weekend."

"Are you trying to make me look like a fool? You and your father..."

"What? Do you think we planned this?"

Larry grabbed an oar and started to paddle on one side of the boat. Liv took the other oar, trying to help.

"No! Sit down."

Liv sat. The afternoon sun scorched her skin. Larry had a thing about her father, maybe because he'd grown up without one. She watched him attack the waves with the wooden oar. It would take hours to get anywhere. A cloud crept across the sun, cooling the breeze. Larry looked like a little boy playing ship's captain, or pirate. She couldn't decide which. Luckily, another boat came along and lent them a tank of gas. Larry helped Liv out of the boat without looking at her, his lips pressed tight, eyes glistening.

She touched his face. "Marry me," she said.

A white boat approaches from the west. The driver waves to Luke, who slides down in his seat, slowing the engine. POLICE, the side of the boat reads. Shit and damn, as Lucy would say. He considers racing away. He'd keep going, out of the harbour, past the breakers, out to the open ocean, until he ran out of gas. And then what? He'd be fish food, that's what. Like his father always said, "Respect the ocean, sport, or you might end up food for the fishes."

Liv sees the infant arms and legs of her children. Lucy's are pudgy and pink. She learned to walk early, making a point of running away whenever she could. Liv watched her toddle down the garden path, yellow curls bobbing, hurling herself at the trunk of the white cedar, arms stretched around it, face looking up into its long limbs, where Larry stood balanced on one fat branch, hammering nails into a board. Luke was there too—four years old, playing on the gravel path, sifting pebbles through his fingers. When he saw Liv, he ran to her and grabbed at her cotton skirt, wiping his constantly running nose on the hem. Liv could not lift him because her arms were full of ripe lemons. She called to Laina, jumping rope with a friend, "Bring me a basket for these lemons, sweetie." Laina dropped the rope and skipped to the house without a word to fetch the basket.

Laina puts away the vacuum cleaner, the dusting rags, the Lemon Pledge, the Windex. The house looks clean and neat. Windows gleam. She has even cleaned the piano keys. In ten days, her grandparents will be here, returned for the holidays from their house in North Carolina, where they'd retired a few years ago, claiming they'd had enough of the island. But Dad had said admiringly, "They made a pretty penny selling that big property of theirs. Now they can buy a nice place Stateside for a third of the price and live on the proceeds. The cost of living is a hell of a lot cheaper over there." Is that why Dad's gone Stateside? The cost of living? Laina's other grandmother had retired to Florida when Laina was a baby, but she'd been American to start with, which made Dad American too, even though he'd been born here. Since he'd never lived in the States, he'd been unable to get U.S. citizenship for his kids. If Laina were American, would he have taken her with him?

She slumps onto the couch, staring at the shiny surface of the coffee table she's just polished. At first she'd dreaded her grandparents' impending arrival, what they'd say when they saw her mother, that they'd take them all away to North Carolina, and Laina would lose her friends. But now that everything is too much, she longs for them to take over. She thinks of phoning to ask them to come sooner, but doesn't know how to say what's the matter with her mother, doesn't know the word to use.

If you look closely at Liv, the only movement you'll notice is her top lip twitching. She's running through the garden with her sister, Carol. Her father lifts them up, one in each arm, so they can pick oranges from the big tree. Her small palm cups an orange, its bulk dropping instantly into her hand, as if it has been waiting for an excuse to fall, or a safe landing place.

Lucy has eaten two lemons. The tart sweet juice has dried on her fingers, leaving them a little sticky. She's picked nasturtiums, roses, and oleander to decorate her tree house. Their colours brighten the shade of the white cedar. She's fetched a blanket, some books, and her stuffed rabbit from the room she shares with Laina. She sits on the blanket, *Alice in Wonderland* in hand, and reads a few pages, looking ahead for the pictures. The Cheshire cat is her favourite, how he disappears around his smile. She also likes the caterpillar's raised eyebrows as he asks, "Whoo Are Yoou?" Lucy is perhaps the least affected by her father's unexplained departure and her mother's depression. Licking her fingers, she turns the page—all those little oysters following the Walrus and the Carpenter. She doesn't feel a bit sorry for them—well, maybe just a bit. She drops the book to pick up her stuffed rabbit. Rubbing his fuzzy belly across her face, she lies down on the blanket. The tree is dry after its late morning shower. The sun peeks in through the thick shiny leaves as it begins to sink behind the oleanders.

Liv lies in her playpen. A yellow bear stares at her. Its eyes are blue buttons. She reaches towards it, noticing her own pink fingers, her small starfish hand. She's caught up in staring at it, until she feels a gnawing, yawning emptiness in her belly, and opens her mouth to cry for food.

Laina, stirring a pot of chicken noodle soup, hears the click of the driveway gate. The spoon falls into the soup. Dad's home! She bolts out the door and up the path to the driveway, but instead of her dad, she sees her brother with a policeman. Luke waves, giving her a sheepish smile.

"Good afternoon, young lady," says the policeman. "Are your parents home?"

Laina feels something small and brittle snap under her stocking feet. She cannot answer the policeman, whose warm, bright smile makes her want to cry. She runs back inside to get her mother.

Lucy hears a man's deep voice in her dreams. "Daddy." She wakes, and rolls over in bed. But the bed slips and splinters, falling out from under her, as she drops past shadowy leaves like feathers stroking the orange sky, until she meets the rain-softened earth with a thump.

Liv steps outside, blinks into the last rays of sunlight, jumps at the sound of the screen door clicking shut. She and Laina are both in time to see the policeman's jacket billow behind him as he and Luke run down the path to the lemon grove. A sour lump of fear rises in Liv's chest. Wrapping her ratty wool cardigan more closely around her, she stumbles after them.

Laina follows her mother. Great warm tears drip down her face as she runs. She feels a rush of emotions that will inundate her dreams for years, but what rises to the top, loosening her arms and legs, is relief.

The policeman reaches Lucy first. Luke crouches beside them, watches him check her pulse with trembling fingers and bend his face close to hers to feel her breath. Luke can hear the rustle of the policeman's jacket and the sigh he makes as he rests back on his heels.

Liv stands under the white cedar, twisting and tugging at one of the leather buttons on her cardigan. She steps forward as the policeman lifts Lucy from the ground, holding her so that Liv can see her face. A round patch of Lucy's cheek is bright yellow. At first Liv feels queasy, thinking a yellow hole has opened into her daughter's face. Then she touches the yellow, discovers she can peel it from Lucy's warm skin. She stares at it, feels its smooth oily surface, presses it to her nose.

What We Hold in Our Hands

"THE MOON'S HOLDING WATER TONIGHT," SAID MY GRAND-mother, Esty. She was gazing out my mother's bay window at the half moon, which lay on its side like a white bowl suspended in the dark. Its light softened the yellow lawns of the Boston suburb, and smoothed the dirty traces of snow.

"I've never heard that expression before," I said, thinking it made the moon into a sponge or a woman's body retaining water.

Esty was starting to be frail. Her shoulders leaned forward to protect a sinking chest. Her pale knuckles trembled as she gripped the arms of her chair, and lowered herself back onto the cushioned seat.

We had just finished eating. My husband Len was in the kitchen helping my mother with the dishes. She always had to wipe away the remains of dinner before we could have dessert. Esty had wanted to dry, but Len had insisted, pressing his palms together in what he thought was a whimsical imitation of prayer, and begging, "Please, Esty. Drying dishes is one of the great pleasures in my life."

Esty had given a dry laugh like a cough. "Well, I wouldn't want to deprive you."

Len liked to make Esty and my mother laugh. Lately his antics never earned more than a grudging smile from me. His need for approval was wearing me out, and I didn't like the way he sought it everywhere, joking with shop clerks and waitresses, wooing his patients into thinking he was wonderful.

"Here's dessert," he said, bearing one of Esty's homemade pumpkin pies into the dining room. My mother followed with teapot and mugs. Len poured the tea while I served the pie.

Looking up from her plate with half a smile, Esty said, "Last night I dreamed I killed a man."

My mother raised her eyebrows and sent me a side-sweeping, I-told-you-so look. She wanted to convince me that Esty was slipping into senility, but although Esty's body was weakening, her mind seemed as sharp and tough as ever. I suspected that my mother's worries were fueled by equal parts dread and desire, like the whiskey and soda she used to pour herself each evening after my father left.

"How did you kill him?" I asked, squeezing lemon into my tea and thinking about the gun Esty kept under her pillow.

"I just beat him with my fists until he fell over dead. He died so easily, he must have been in pretty bad shape."

At my grandfather Gus's funeral, Esty had thrown herself onto his body during the viewing, kissing him and crying like a little girl. I'd never seen her show him such affection when he was alive, not so much as a peck or a hug. They were always arguing or teasing each other. Sometimes he'd kiss her cheek, causing her to squirm and hiss an exasperated *Oh, Gus!*

At the funeral, I'd felt as though I was spying through the window of my grandparents' bedroom as they lay in their queen-size bed, Esty peeling the blanket from Gus's pyjama-clad body while she snuggled close, her fingers wandering down his white buttons.

"Did you know the man in your dream?" I asked.

"He was just some man. I don't know where he came from."

"Are you sure there was nothing familiar about him?"

Esty shook her head.

"Karyl," Len said in his don't-go-there voice, placing a hand on my shoulder.

"Len." I mimicked his tone, pushed his hand away.

Len and I had laboured through the fall, dealing with an

outbreak of flu and pre-Christmas neuroses. Our office handled people's physical and emotional ailments, Len as homeopath, me as social worker. But the same clients who couldn't get enough of his little white pills and hearty advice eyed me with suspicion when I encouraged them to talk about their troubles, or recommended books for them to read.

"The man in your dream wasn't Dad, was he?" my mother asked Esty.

"Of course not. I could never hurt your father, not even in a dream."

"Maybe you were trying to shut him up." My mother sliced another piece of pie for herself. "You always said he talked too much."

Esty had been secretary and receptionist for Gus's small-town medical practice. He'd collected stories about everyone in town, sharing them with her, but she'd never let him repeat them to others. If patients had thought their secrets unsafe, they'd have visited the doctor in the next town, or the young man who'd moved into the old florist's shop.

"Mom's right," I said to Esty. "Whenever Grandpa started to tell me a story, even stories about his childhood, you'd always ask me to help with some chore."

"Like hanging laundry," my mother said.

"Or filling Grandpa's birdfeeders."

"I don't remember that." Esty smoothed her paper napkin with both hands and folded it in two.

"Do you remember the story of the schoolteacher with the dreadful secret?" I asked. "I never did find out what happened to her."

Esty shrugged.

My mother scraped the filling out of her pastry, which lay wan and limp on her plate.

When I was small, Gus used to lift me off the floor and twirl me around while Esty yelled, "Watch out for the furniture!" He'd make a quarter disappear, then reemerge behind my ear or under my chin. Rolling her eyes, Esty would say, "I'd like to see you make my shingles disappear. Some doctor."

My mother stuck her fork into the empty crust, poked a series of holes across its surface. "I could always rely on Dad to take my side, to let me go out and enjoy myself," she said to Esty. "You seemed to think that life was just about work and school."

"We were brought up to work hard."

"More tea?" Len filled my mug before I had a chance to say yes.

When he topped up my mother's tea, she leaned her cheek against his hand.

By the time I was ten or eleven, I squirmed away from Gus whenever he tried to pick me up or pull a quarter from my ear. Since my father no longer showed me such attentions, I chose to think myself too old, to regard hugs and playfulness as insults to my autonomy. Rejecting their inadequate consolation, I'd ignore Gus the way Esty did, while she and I logged hand after hand of Gin Rummy, or dashed outside with a handful of carrots to feed the neighbour's horses.

Back then, my parents often went out to dinner parties, or had people over to play bridge or dance on our scuffed living room floor. Even when the party took place in our own home, I was sometimes sent to sleep at Esty and Gus's. But during my early teens, the parties had ended, and my mother had ordered moss-green wall-to-wall carpeting to be laid down over the living room parquet. Later I learned that my father had been sleeping with one of the women in their group of friends.

"Does anyone want to go for a walk?" Len asked.

"It's too cold." I pressed the warm mug to my cheek.

"We could play cards," my mother said.

"My father used to play the piano after dinner." Esty sighed. "Those were good times."

"I thought you hated those old days," I said. "Your mother

working herself to death, your father unable to hold a job. It doesn't sound like much fun."

"Oh, but my sisters and I made our own fun, naming the chickens, making dolls out of rags and corn cobs, singing around the piano. When my father was in a good mood, he sang the most comical songs."

I tried to catch my mother's eye, to confirm what I remembered her saying about Esty's father—that he used to beat them. But she rose from her chair without looking at me and disappeared into the kitchen.

"What happened when your father was in a bad mood?" I asked.

"Oh, he used to storm and shout and go off for the day, sometimes longer."

"Where did he work?" asked Len.

"He worked on the railroad or cutting timber, but mostly he was between jobs. He couldn't get along with his bosses. There was always a fight. He wasn't a bad man, just unhappy."

Esty seemed to have forgotten her old feelings about her childhood, whatever had led her, for most of her life, to avoid mentioning those days, and to stop Gus from talking about them too. Now the past was wiped clean, allowed into the ether of her fresh consciousness, as if she'd gotten religion. Maybe her mind really wasn't as sharp and tough as it used to be.

My mother returned from the kitchen with a bottle of peach schnapps and some glasses.

"Now that was a good idea," Len said, taking a glass.

"I thought we could use a little something."

"Tell us more about your dream, Grandma." Convinced that the man in Esty's dream had been her father, I wanted her to see it too.

"There's nothing more to tell. All I remember is beating at this strange man until he fell over as if he'd been struck by lightning. Struck down dead. And he never fought back, didn't even try to get away."

"I've had that dream myself," my mother said. "But I know who the man was."

We all knew who the man was—*my* father, Derek, who had remarried years ago and died of cancer early this spring.

I allowed Len to grip my fingers under the table. He'd wanted to spend the holidays in the Dominican Republic where we could have lingered in bed over champagne and sliced pineapple, catching up on our lovemaking.

Yesterday, driving here from our home in Toronto, we'd found ourselves on the wrong road and stopped for coffee at the next exit. Dusk had begun to set in, the sky spitting snowflakes.

"I don't like the look of this weather." Len had tugged on my scarf. "Let's get our coffee to go."

"Can't we just sit here for ten minutes?"

"We have at least an hour ahead of us, and I don't want to drive it in a snowstorm."

"There's not going to be a snowstorm," I said, choosing a booth beside the window, trying to ignore the rhythmic tapping of Len's fingers against the Formica tabletop, trying to pretend that I was enjoying my bitter coffee and cold apple pie.

He stirred two sugars into his mug. "Isn't it interesting how you're doing your best to put off arriving at your mother's house? Especially since the whole trip was your idea."

"Stop it, Len."

"All I'm saying is we should have gone south for a real holiday."

"Mom says Esty's not well. It might be her last Christmas."

"I thought you didn't believe your mother's doom and gloom."

"What if it's true?" I'd pressed the hot mug to my face. "I never got to see my father before he died, didn't even know he was sick."

"It's natural for you to feel angry." Len lowered his eyebrows, assuming the compassionate tone he used with his patients.

"I'm not angry. I'm grieving."

Without Len, I would never have completed my Social Work

degree. Disabled by depression, deserted by the boyfriend I'd followed to Canada, I'd been ready to quit school when a friend had recommended a homeopath, who'd turned out to be Len. He'd lent me a light visor and prescribed a regimen of herbs and vitamins, but it had been his attention and care that had pulled me through.

My mother poured herself more of the awful peach schnapps.

"It sounds like you're still angry at Karyl's father," Len said.

"It doesn't keep me up nights."

"Do we have to talk about this?" I pulled my fingers away from Len's grip.

"Talking is good," he said.

"I hate talking. No wonder I'm such a lousy therapist."

"You have to stop saying that." His warning tone again.

In the morning, we'd picked up Esty, who'd been waiting in the kitchen with her overnight bag. The neighbouring meadow where we used to feed the horses had been sold long ago, and now bore a brick bungalow with a red door, but Gus's birdfeeders still hung from the apple tree in the backyard, and inside, the place still smelled of pot roast and soap. When I was a child, I used to burst through the door after a few weeks' absence, delighted to find the same brown leather couch, the same board games in the cupboard, the same violets growing in their painted pots, and Esty and Gus in their usual places, bent over a puzzle at the kitchen table. But this morning, all the familiar objects and smells had made me squeeze my face tight to stop the tears that threatened to undo me.

"It's too bad you don't enjoy your work, Karyl," Esty said.

"That's rich coming from you," my mother said. "You never thought that work was something to enjoy."

"Oh, I liked my work well enough, but most aren't so lucky. Remember how much Derek hated his law practice? I bet that was what made him go off the rails."

"You always said it was my fault. That he got bored with me." My mother looked down at her empty glass.

"He was a restless one," Esty said. "Trying to 'find himself.' Trying to forget himself more likely."

Ever since my father left us, I'd been trying to forget him, forget how remote he'd become when he was still at home, forget the way he used to tuck me into bed when I was small, answering the stream of questions I invented to make him linger by my side. Forget the way I used to help him in the garden, digging holes for the tomato and cucumber seedlings. He'd shown me how to tamp down the soil around them, how to stake the plants when they grew bigger, how to pinch off the new growth between the established branches and the stalk. He was always giving me some vegetable nickname.

"Look, Peapod," he'd say, pointing to the fine green seedlings that had appeared beside a row of onions. "You planted those last week. Remember?"

"Are those the carrots?" I'd ask, squatting beside him.

"Yes. And when they get a little bigger, you're in charge of thinning them. All you have to do is pull some out to make them less crowded. I'll let you know when it's time."

"Okay." I'd jump up and wrap my arms around his neck.

Squinting into the distance, he'd rise slowly, making my legs leave the ground.

"Don't drop me," I'd cry, seeking safety in the belief that he never would.

Len wanted me to remember these and other, harder things— how my father's gardening phase hadn't lasted two summers, how I'd felt excluded from his later hobbies and sudden passions, like learning to fly an airplane or photographing blurry horizons. I used to skip rope in the basement for what seemed like hours, waiting for him to emerge from the darkroom he'd built. Sometimes I'd give up and go outside into the fierce sunlight, playing hopscotch on the paving stones that cut across his abandoned garden.

I gave Len a somber, apologetic smile.

He grinned back, ever hopeful. "How about that walk?"

"We already had a walk today. Remember?"

We'd navigated the twisting suburban streets, our heads bowed to the wind, walking silently, our arms a swinging bridge between us, until he'd said, "I'm worried about you."

"Well, don't worry." I'd stuffed my hands into my pockets. "I'll be fine. I'm not one of your patients."

Len believed that unreleased emotions festered inside of us, spawning disease, that our bodies were fluid, and if we kept our emotions moving, we could transform ourselves, creating whatever reality we desired. Only, most of our clients either *couldn't* do this, or didn't want to. Perhaps they sensed my own lack of faith in Len's theories.

"I thought we were going to play cards," Esty said.

"We are," said my mother.

Len, who hated card games, yawned and rose from his chair. "Since no one wants to walk, I guess I'll go see what's on TV."

"Maybe Grandma will tell us one of Grandpa's old stories," I said, feeling a sudden panic at the thought of Len going, reaching out a hand to stop him. I wanted to be able to count on him to never leave me, even though I sometimes felt the urge to leave him, to pack up and go somewhere I'd never been, eyeing the distant horizon.

"What about the schoolteacher with the dreadful secret?" I asked Esty.

"That was so long ago," she said.

"It sounds like a good one," Len encouraged her.

"Let me see if I can remember. I want to get the story right, like he would have told it."

"It won't be the same," my mother said.

"I'd like to hear it anyway." Len was standing behind me, working his fingers into my knotted shoulder muscles.

"That feels good," I said, wishing I could always respond this way to his touch.

"The schoolteacher's name was May Starling," Esty said. "I remember her name because she had a face like a bird's—delicate features, but her nose stood out like a beak. She wore her blonde hair in a bun and was pretty in a tall, gangly way. She came into the waiting room very standoffish, hardly spoke to me, just sat primly on her seat until Gus was ready to see her. I don't think she knew we were married. Some people didn't. New people mostly. Later I asked Gus about her, and this is what he told me:

"She sat on the other side of his desk and stared at him for what must have been close on a minute, then said, 'You look like a trustworthy man.'

He said, 'I try to be.'

She leaned in closer. 'I'm in perfect health, but I need to talk to someone.'

'People often come here to talk about their problems,' Gus said.

'I have a dreadful secret,' she confessed. 'And it's wearing me down not to be able to tell anyone.'

'You can tell me,' he offered, laying his hand flat on the desk so that she could touch it if she wanted, if that would help her to get the story out.

She placed her hand close to his, but not touching, and said, 'Last fall, when I was new to the school, I came in one morning to find a grown man sitting in one of the small chairs. He wasn't one of the other teachers so I thought he must be a father come to talk about his child, but he wasn't that either. He said he worked on the train, and he'd taken my ticket when I was moving here. He said I looked as if I'd been crying, which I probably had been, as I was sad to be leaving home and nervous about my new job. He'd stayed in the same car as long as he could, watching me, deciding he wanted to marry me. Later, at the station, he asked who I was and where I was staying. As he told me this, his dark eyes seemed to burn through mine, and his long fingers gripped the back of the chair. He stood up to grab hold of me and kiss me. I kissed him back. I could have stood there all day kissing him, but I knew my students would soon be arriving, and I couldn't allow myself to be found in such a position. So I broke away and said, *I can't marry you,* even though I thought I might like to if I had some time to get to know him. But he cursed me and pushed over the chair. I was afraid he might hurt me, but he sloped off out the door. The children came in. And the day carried on in the usual manner.

'I never saw him again. I wanted to, but I didn't know where to find him. When I asked at the train station, they said he'd quit his job. Then a few weeks ago, I saw his ghost in my classroom. It was early morning before the children arrived, the same time he'd come before. I turned around from the blackboard, where I'd been writing a poem for the class, and saw him sitting in the same chair. But when I ran to him, he vanished.

'And you see, I'm confused. I don't know if it was a real ghost or just my longing for him. I don't know if he died for love of me like in some old song, or if I'm just imagining this whole thing. And I don't know what's wrong with me. How could I have such feelings about a man I hardly know, a man so irrational, maybe even insane?'

"Gus tried to pat her hand where she'd left it on the desk, only now it was a fist, the knuckles white and trembling. He told her she needed to forget about this man whether he was a ghost or alive. She needed to get out with other young people, to go dancing, play cards or tennis. He prescribed a sedative to help her sleep. She thanked him, pressing his hand with her cold thin fingers, and left.

"Gus told me all this shaking his head, not knowing what to make of it. I told him, 'She's a fine one to be teaching our children. There's something not right about her.' A year later, when the doctor from the next town came for a visit, we discovered that this May Starling had told him her dreadful secret too. So Gus called the new doctor in town, and sure enough, she'd been to see him as well. She'd been running around collecting prescriptions. 'An addict,' I said. 'Or maybe she just likes the sympathy,' said Gus. The new doctor was convinced that she really believed her story, that she'd imagined the whole incident out of loneliness. But when she walked out of Gus's office that day, there was defiance in her smile and a flicker of something that said she'd gotten what she wanted."

Esty's eyes were bright and clear, her face flushed.

"Wow," Len said. "I'd like to hear some more of Gus's old stories."

My mother shifted in her chair. "That's not the story Dad used to tell. You've changed it."

"It needed a little doctoring." Esty gave her dry, cough-like laugh.

"Grandpa told me she had brown hair like mine." He'd also told me that she'd held onto his hand the whole time she was telling her story, her fingers trembling inside of his.

"Gus's memory wasn't always the best."

"I feel sorry for that May Starling," Len said.

"May Starling!" my mother snorted. "That wasn't even her name. She was a teacher in my school. Her name was May Shaw. She was crazy as a loon and beat our hands with a big ruler whenever she could get away with it."

"How come I never heard any of this before?" I asked.

"I didn't think anyone was interested in those old stories," Esty said.

My mother screwed the lid onto the bottle of schnapps. "Let the dead lie is my motto."

"I guess my father is the exception."

"Your father was always the exception."

I thought of my father lying sick in a Seattle hospital. His wife had called to say that he'd died of an aggressive liver cancer. They'd only discovered it a few weeks before it killed him. I'd thanked her for calling, but cursed her afterwards, hating her for not thinking to call me sooner, hating him for dying, for leaving me, hating myself for not having tried harder to keep in touch.

When Gus had died, my mother had invited Esty to live with her, but she'd wanted to stay in her own house. She still slept in the queen-size bed she'd shared with Gus all those years, but now she had a new companion—a small black Beretta she kept under her pillow to help her feel safe. I wondered if she'd be able to use it if she needed to. Her movements were prone to sudden pauses. Even though her mind was sharp, sometimes a glitch in her brain's ability to remember where it wanted to go could strand her body for seconds at a time, making her feel lost and weak.

What power she must have felt in her dream to be able to kill a man so easily, to beat away the memory of her cruel father, replacing him with one who was kinder and well-meaning, just as she'd done when she'd married Gus, leaving behind the harshness of her childhood for his friendly embrace.

"What about that card game?" Esty asked.

"I think I'll call it a night." Len raised his hand in a parting salute.

"I'll be there in a few minutes," I called after him.

"There's always time for a quick game of Gin." My mother pulled the cards from their box. "Feeling lucky, Ma?"

"Luck has very little to do with it."

"Grandpa used to say he was born lucky," I said.

As the youngest of eight children, Gus hadn't been needed to help on the farm so he'd been free to finish school and proceed to college on a scholarship. After med school, he'd come home to marry his high school sweetheart, Esty, who'd had trouble accepting her good fortune, which must have felt alien and undeserved. She'd spent the rest of her life knocking wood and throwing salt over her shoulder.

Some of that salt must have blown into my mother's eyes, blinding her, affecting her judgment when it came to choosing a husband. My father had been a good-looking man. In photos he looks tanned and healthy, even in winter, and his grey eyes are wide and dreamy, causing me to wonder what he was thinking.

Esty has a photo of my father and me. He's sitting on the steps of her house, staring into the camera, a kite held loosely in one hand while I hold onto the other. My toddler self is leaning in the direction I want to take him, and our arms create a single line pointing that way. Looking at that picture, I always want him to get up from the steps and follow me, although I can tell from his indolent, sun-struck gaze that he has no intention of rising. Still I imagine myself leading him to my favourite destination, the meadow. The horses stand in the shimmering grasses like creatures from a fairy story. They lower their heads to chew the tall clover. The sun warms their dark flanks. My father lifts me so that I can touch their lustrous coats, which look richer and more enticing than chocolate. He holds me in his arms, making me feel safe, even though one horse's big eyeball glistens only a few inches from mine, and its yellow teeth are bared.

Len thought that he could remedy whatever was wrong in my life, just as he'd fixed things for me when we first met, just as he treated his patients, certain that he knew what was best for all of us. But how could he know? How could I? I didn't even know what my grandmother was feeling; instead I saw shadows from my own life playing over her face. The assumption that I could help anyone with their singular pain seemed as illusory to me as Gus's old magic tricks, designed to dazzle and distract, to win applause and approval.

Perhaps my mother was right that the man in Esty's dream had been Gus, telling his stories, charming his patients, performing his tricks of appearance and disappearance like a child playing peek-a-boo.

"Gin!" Esty fanned out her full hand.

My mother tossed her cards onto the table. "You always win."

Esty seemed to hold all the luck that my mother was missing, but she'd brought her up to think that it was skill and cleverness she lacked. When my father left, she'd accused her of letting herself go. And I had blamed her too, when I wasn't blaming myself.

I got up from the table, rested a hand on my mother's shoulder, and let my chin brush the top of her head, where the grey was growing back in. "See you in the morning," I said.

"Goodnight, Karyl." She touched my hand as I moved away.

While Len was brushing his teeth, I pulled on my coat and slipped outside to see the stars. I thought of Esty's story—how May Starling had summoned up a stranger out of her need to be loved, then, without effort or malice, imagined his death as a way of simplifying his love, keeping it as straight and pure as an arrow.

The dark sky showed off its darts of light, but Esty's moon stood out like a fist holding secrets, holding our frozen love and buried dreams, our helplessness and anger, so white it made my knuckles burn.

Compact

GILDA'S YOUNGER SISTER, TONI, IS DYING. THE CANCER launched in her ovaries a year ago. Now, even after radiation and chemotherapy, it has conquered her blood, infiltrated her bones, broken down hips, pelvis, spine.

Gilda sits by Toni's bed, watching her sister's breath, convinced she can see it stir the dimly lit air, air perfumed by two dozen stalwart daffodils she bought to replace the drooping rosebuds from Toni's husband, Michael. Last week he moved into the guestroom where he can sleep without fear of rolling over and crushing Toni, who, only a year ago, was teaching spin classes and Pilates at one of Gilda and Ed's health clubs.

Moonlight settles on Toni's smoothly gleaming head, and forty-one years collapse beneath Gilda, who remembers her baby sister's golden fuzz of hair, the smile that had seemed like a secret shared between the two of them, the fullness that had flooded her eleven-year-old chest, how the word, "love," had become real, a warmth she could feel in her blood, on her skin.

Although married for several years, Toni and Michael have chosen not to have children, a decision that used to trouble Gilda, but now seems like a blessing.

"I have your kids," Toni used to say.

"But they're growing up. Soon they won't be around much."

"Still it's fun to see what they'll do."

"Fun for you maybe."

Gilda's four children are old enough to vote, and have all, one after the other, found their own ways to disappoint or alarm her.

Josh is living with the wrong woman, Jenny dating the wrong man, Lisa pursuing the wrong career—modelling—she's pretty but what chance does she have? While Robin, her youngest, is in the wrong university—a three-hour drive away—and never answers when Gilda calls. Her husband, Ed, is in the wrong too. Lately, he can do nothing right, but has yet to stop trying. His patience, so scarce when they were younger, has grown in step with Gilda's impatience, threatening to calm and console her when what she wants most is to cling to the comforting weight of her anger and sorrow.

"Gil," Toni whispers.

Her labouring voice pulls Gilda close.

"I'm here."

"I don't want you to feel angry about this. Promise."

"What do you mean?" Gilda wants to grab Toni's words and squeeze the meaning out of them.

"Don't blame everyone when I die. Don't take it personally like you always do."

Toni's eyes open to reveal a sly flicker.

"What do you mean always? When have I ever lost my only sister?"

"You get angry and withdraw. I don't want you to do that because of me. Promise."

"Isn't anger one of the stages of grief?"

"Just promise, or I'll pinch you like I used to."

"Okay, I promise. But you're not dead yet."

The next morning, after Ed has left for work, Gilda is drinking coffee in her terry bathrobe and weeping over the Sports section (Toni is a Blue Jays' fan) when her best friend, Carol, knocks at the kitchen door.

"I'm taking you shopping." Carol drops her leather and gilt purse onto the table and fills a mug from the coffee pot.

"Can't. I have to sit with Toni." Gilda clings to the newspaper.

"Let the nurse take care of her. Just for today."

"But the injections are buying us time. I don't want to waste it shopping."

"You won't be any good for Toni if you have a nervous breakdown."

Gilda's grip on the paper tightens. She wants to strike her friend with it, to mess up her tidy blonde do and crisp ivory collar, but Carol gives her a small sad smile and reaches for her free hand.

"Okay." Gilda releases the baseball news.

"Now go put on something nice," Carol orders.

Her bossiness and Gilda's angry responses used to cause brief but bitter fractures in their long friendship, but they've managed to outgrow that old pattern, gaining faith in each other's fondness and loyalty. And, although Gilda would never admit it, lately she has begun to find comfort in being told what to do.

In the shoe department at Holt's, Carol pulls Gilda away from the shiny black loafers she's been eyeing.

"You have a pair of those already. You need something new, something Ed will like."

"You're nuts. Ed doesn't care about my shoes."

"He'll care about these." Carol dangles a pink sandal with three-inch heels.

Gilda shakes her head.

"We'll each buy a pair and get the guys to take us out for dinner."

"I wouldn't enjoy myself."

"I hate to see you put your life on hold because Toni's sick. I'm afraid you'll forget how to start up again afterwards."

"Afterwards?"

"Sorry, sweetheart." Carol pushes the pink shoe at her. "You'd have loved them in the old days."

When they used to babysit Toni, she'd kept them busy playing beauty pageant in her mother's high heels and her own lacy party dresses, pulling evening gowns and shoes from their mother's closet for Gilda and Carol to try. The gowns had been tight on Gilda, who'd had to make do with fringed shawls, silk scarves, and beads, while Carol had slipped into the fitted dresses and zipped them up like they'd been made for her. But Gilda had inherited her mother's small feet, so the delicate pumps and sandals had always fit her best.

"Okay. I'll try them."

A sleek young man brings Gilda the sandals in a size six. They are too wide and look ridiculous with her black pantsuit. She tries some turquoise sling-backs and a pair of white wedges that tie around the ankles. Then she finds the red shoes. They're like a pair from her mother's old closet, with slender heels and pointed toes that make the uppers look like red triangles. The forgiving pleated edge of the triangle accommodates her high arch while the backs hug her heels without slipping or cutting into her skin.

"These are better. I don't feel like I'm trying too hard in these. We're not teenagers anymore."

"No kidding." Carol is considering her own feet in a pair of apple-green sandals.

"Don't worry. You're still drop-dead gorgeous." Gilda can't help feeling oversized around Carol, as if she's been cut from too bulky a remnant of material.

As they step stiletto-heeled along Bloor, Carol says, "Give me your purse."

"What for?"

"Just give it to me. I want to put something in it. A surprise."

Gilda shrugs, handing her red bag to Carol, who picks through the contents.

"Aha!" She flourishes Gilda's old black compact before dropping it into a garbage bin at the side of the road.

"What did you do that for?"

"It was so old you could've gotten a disease. Look. I bought you a new one."

Carol slides a silver compact from the pocket of her beige trench.

Gilda is used to her friend's impulsive behaviour, her oddly expressed generosity.

"It's nice," she says. The gift feels smooth and cool in her hand, but heavier than she expected. The lid is inlaid with mother-of-pearl and onyx in the shape of an elephant with an uplifted trunk.

"That's good luck," Carol says.

Gilda flips open the compact. In the magnifying mirror, her nose is red and splotchy from the March wind, narrow gaps appear in the black line edging her lids, and the delicate skin there is puffy and green from not sleeping, but her eyes look bright enough, still the same inexplicable blue, shared by no one else in her family.

"Come on." Carol grabs her arm.

Gilda's ankles wobble a little, making her feel like a kid parading around her parents' pink and aqua bedroom. It was Carol's idea to wear their purchases out of the store, their old shoes tucked into new boxes inside crisp shopping bags. Now they're going to the Four Seasons for afternoon tea—also Carol's idea.

In the hotel lobby, an enormous marble vase overflows with red and yellow striped parrot tulips, yellow lilies, and pussy willows.

"Spring," says Gilda, sticking her nose inside a tulip, sniffing its subtle perfume. "Toni would love these. Maybe we could bring her here."

"Just for today no talk about Toni, okay? Tomorrow you can buy her all the tulips you want."

They order a full tea, their Darjeeling and Earl Grey arriving along with a three-tiered dish full of goodies. Gilda pops a miniature roast beef sandwich into her mouth. Chewing slowly, she feels the fragrant heat of fresh horseradish rise through her nostrils. She thinks of Toni—how they used to grate the root for Easter dinner, laughing together as their eyes streamed, how she'd take a bite of horseradish and pretend to be choking on it so that Toni could come to her rescue with a glass of ice water.

"Michael didn't get home until eight o'clock last night," she says, twisting her linen napkin.

"He just can't deal with it. Don't be so hard on him."

Michael is working longer hours than usual. He comes home, briefcase full, eyes dull and unblinking as if they've been switched off at their source.

What is it about the Taylor sisters' husbands? Why do they go along for years—attentive, devoted even—then fizzle out like defective fireworks?

Two and a half years ago, Ed took Gilda out for an expensive dinner so he could tell her that he didn't love her anymore. Red wine, *foie gras*, and filet mignon to ease the blow. Sobbing, she threw it all up in the ladies' room. Why couldn't he have told her at home over a bowl of soup?

Ed has recovered from his midlife upheaval, but Gilda still holds it against him. Forgiveness has never been one of her strengths. He tries hard to redeem himself, teaching her to golf, planning weekend trips, but whenever he tells her that she looks beautiful or he loves her, she slaps on a distant little smile like a reflective shield, prepared for the next time.

Since Toni's illness, Gilda's relationship with her own body, always troubled, has become even more estranged. Everything about it repulses her, from the fleshy pads of her thumbs, the skin loosening under her chin, and the pouches of fat under her arms, to the solid curves of her calves, the ample rounds of her breasts, and the cellulite dimples on her bum. She should have been the one to get sick. She is older, eats too many chips and desserts, and although she works in the business, never spends time in the gym. So why Toni? Why not her? Wouldn't the cancer cells thrive on Gilda's discontent and self-loathing? If only she could stand in for her sister like a sacrificial lamb, paint her own healthy, plentiful blood on Toni's doorway.

Carol pours Gilda more Earl Grey. Gilda takes a sip, feels her body sink into the armchair.

"She stopped breathing last night."

Toni had started awake on a noisy in-breath.

"Gil," she said. "Remember our pet rabbits?"

"Stinky and Bowling Ball?"

"Remember when Stinky died and Bowling Ball developed an insatiable appetite?"

"He got rounder and rounder." Gilda laughed.

Toni was laughing too, her body shuddering, her breath sharp and raspy.

"It hurts." She reached for Gilda's hand.

Gilda found herself wiping away her own tears with the hand holding Toni's, causing the two of them to start laughing all over again.

"Have a scone." Carol drops one onto Gilda's plate.

Gilda picks up the heavy silver butter knife, which slips from her unsteady fingers. Bending to retrieve it, she catches sight of the red shoes. They seem to have arrived fresh from another era, the costume of a vanished and hopeful self. She tries to wiggle her toes, but even though they can hardly move inside of the neat red triangles, they don't feel uncomfortable.

Returning the knife to the table, she says, "I should be at work today."

"You need a break. Everything will be fine without you."

"The funny thing is, the less I work, the less I feel like myself. But I don't miss it. I'm not sure I even want to go back."

"Maybe you've had enough."

Ed had tried to explain his declaration of lapsed love. "It was one of those things that as soon as I said it, I didn't feel that way anymore." His smile had been somber and lonesome.

Gilda looks down at the red shoes. "Toni says I take things personally and get angry."

"You do," Carol says. "You're touchy."

"How did I manage to keep *you* as a friend all these years?"

"I know you'd do anything for me." Carol slices a chocolate tart in two. "Do you want half?"

"No, you eat it."

"Come on, chocolate triggers endorphins."

Gilda lays her napkin over her plate.

Zipping up her mouth is one way to shun the things of this world that Toni is leaving behind. Gilda will be here to love them for a good many years more, to love roast beef and scones, tulips and new shoes, to love Ed and the kids, no matter how angry and afraid she feels that her children no longer need her, that they've left her behind, and Ed could leave too.

Her parents died four years ago, within six months of each other. They always said that family was the most important thing, shelter from a hostile world. They'd counted on Gilda to hold the family together, to keep the old traditions like Sunday dinners, but since their deaths, she has gradually given up trying. Her kids always have somewhere else to go. Next week will be Easter. Carol has invited them all to her house after church, but Robin has to study for exams, Josh is in England meeting his girlfriend's parents, and Jenny has yet to return Gilda's phone call. So far, only Lisa is coming. Gilda knows that she will have to get used to a smaller household. Maybe it does not mean a smaller life.

"My shoes are pinching," Carol says.

"Mine are amazingly comfortable. Do you really think Ed will like them?"

"He'll go nuts." Carol empties the remaining drops from her teapot. "Should we ask for more hot water?"

"No, it's getting late. I'm going to the ladies'."

Washing her hands, Gilda peers into the mirror where her features are their normal size, her cheeks no longer red. She pulls out her new compact, flips open the lid, and examines her face in the magnifying mirror. Her skin is pale pink, textured with a weave of lines and pores, her nose luminous with soft down, and, from her dark pupils, golden stripes radiate outward like petals amongst the several shades of blue. When she powders her nose, cheeks, and chin, grains of talc cling to the fine hairs, like the powder she sprinkled on Toni's bare bum when she was a baby. Toni had been free from diaper rash, cradle cap, colic—all ailments Gilda had suffered, according to their mother. Toni, small and perfect with soft pink skin and blonde curls, had toddled around in the lacy dresses their father bought her, giggling deeply from her belly at the faces Gilda pulled for her. When their mother, who'd thought she'd never have another child, had called Toni a blessing from God, eleven-year-old Gilda had felt the truth of it in her throat, along with the bitter knowledge that her own birth had not been greeted with the same sense of wonder and gratitude.

A month ago, when her sister was still able to walk, Gilda took her to their favourite diner for lunch. Toni ordered her regular, the tuna salad plate, Gilda, a club sandwich with fries.

Toni was wearing the blue and grey knit cap that hid her baldness and made her look wide-eyed and elfin. "It was good to see Ed last night," she said. "You never bring him around anymore. I was beginning to think he was squeamish."

"Ed's always happy to see you, in sickness and in health."

"You should be nicer to him."

"What do you mean?"

"You're always putting him down. He's a good husband. He loves you."

"Sure." Gilda squeezed her paper napkin into a tight little pellet.

"He does. I can tell. You should be nicer."

"I should be a lot of things I guess."

"I'm sorry, Gil. You're always so good to me. I know you'd do anything."

"I would," she said, smoothing the napkin.

But, facing the ladies' room mirror, Gilda knows that although she would happily shed her own life for Toni, letting go of everything and everyone who will eventually, and inevitably, be lost to her, she will not be able to keep the promise she's made. Not even Toni, with all the ice water in the world, can soothe the fear and sorrow that stir Gilda's lungs, or sweeten the bitter taste in her mouth.

Flickers

MA WON'T TAKE ME DOWNTOWN TO HEAR JULIE SING. A smoke-filled bar is not her kind of place. I bang my head against the back of my wheelchair.

She says, "Michelle, you're acting like a two year old."

I'm nineteen and, as Ma says, getting older every day.

I stare at the fish tank she bought for my birthday. It sits on a table in a corner of the living room. "You always wanted a pet," she said, filling the tank with water. The next day, she bought eleven neon tetras—silver with splashes of red on their sides and spreading into their tails. They dart through water as if they have someplace urgent to go that changes every few seconds. Watching them makes me tired. Besides, they're not real pets, not like a dog or a cat, someone you could be friends with.

When we first moved into this apartment, I hated it. It's on an ugly street lined with strip malls and car dealerships. If you drive a mile in any direction, that's pretty much all you'll see. The building's a squat, brown rectangle, the elevator lurches and creaks, and everything smells of old meatloaf. But since Julie moved in with Jim next door, living here hasn't been so bad.

Julie sings with a band. She's the woman I wanted to become—fearless, friendly, beautiful in a tough, carefree way, dashing through life like a fish absorbing air from water.

Jim is the drummer with shoulder-length black hair, soft not oily, an Abraham Lincoln beard, long black coat over T-shirt and jeans. He's as tall as Julie is short, with big, fluid-moving limbs.

The day I met Julie, Ma had rolled me into the hallway for my daily change of scene while she cleaned the apartment. I stared at the scuffed grey walls, sniffed the stuffy air that smelled of canned soup, shut my ears to the muffled roar of the vacuum. Then Jim's door burst open. A woman leaped out like a rock star taking the stage. She noticed me right away, her big smile splitting wider.

"Howdy," she said.

Masses of wavy hair streaked yellow and orange haloed her small face. She strode toward me in red cowboy boots. Her jeans bore a big silver belt buckle. Jim lumbered behind her like a horse being led.

"I'm Shel."

"How do you like it here, Shel?" she asked.

"It sucks."

Her laughter overflowed the hall.

"I've seen worse," she said.

I kept staring, amazed that she'd been able to make out my words—my first conversation in three years with anyone other than Ma or the speech therapist. One of the things I lost in the accident was my voice. Inside I can hear the words clearly, but my tongue has trouble forming the sounds, and I have to concentrate to force them out of my throat. Exposed to air, they seem to fall apart. From years of practice, Ma knows how to put the words back together. Julie can hear them before they even leave my mouth.

Ma wheeled me back inside, saying, "Don't get friendly with those two. His father's a surgeon. Would you believe it? Wasting his father's money on drugs and that slut."

"Bitch," I said.

This time, she didn't understand me, or pretended not to.

Julie and I sit outside the apartment building, where there's a patch of grass, a bench, and a few scraggly yellow pansies in a cement planter. We watch Ma hurry down the sidewalk toward the No Frills, stopping for a moment to turn and frown at us. I can tell that she's already sorry she agreed to let me sit in the fresh air with Julie instead of waiting by myself inside.

"How old's your mom?"

Ma is leaning into the wind, which blows her greying hair straight back and billows up inside her big navy windbreaker.

My short dark hair shivers a little, even though Julie and I are sitting in the shelter of a brick wall.

"Early forties?" is the best I can come up with.

"She could be a looker if she'd do something with that hair and those clothes." Julie smooths her own hair, lights a cigarette.

Watching the smoke twist around itself, I remember the doughnut shop where Zack and I used to drink coffee late at night before Ma gave up on my curfew. I always felt more pleased than guilty, thinking how she and I were separated by half a city—me rubbing Zack's knee in a smoky booth downtown, while Ma waited up, watching movies in our grey bungalow. Now I wonder why she didn't have a boyfriend of her own. When I was in grade school, a few men came around, but none stayed long enough for me to notice when they were gone. Ma said they weren't worth the aggravation.

"What's your mother like?" I ask Julie.

"I don't have one." She tosses her cigarette stub onto the soil around the pansies.

"You can have mine," I say.

"I left home when I was sixteen." Julie reaches into her jacket for another cigarette. She strikes a match on the rim of the cement planter, takes a drag. I breathe in as deeply as I can, wanting to suck in all that fragrant smoke, which smells like freedom.

When I was sixteen, I dropped out of school and found a job

in a used record store where I met Zack. He used to bring in old vinyl LP's he'd bought cheap at garage sales or picked out of someone's trash.

"How much for these?" he asked, dark eyes unblinking through the strands of his dirty-blond hair.

"They don't look like much," I said.

"Give me twenty bucks for the lot, and I'll give you a ride home after work." Zack played guitar in an alternative band. I didn't like his music, but I loved tearing down the highway on the back of his bike. He was twenty-seven, listened exclusively to Grunge, and didn't believe that Kurt Cobain's death had been a suicide. Often when I was lying in his bed after we made love, and he was stretched on his back, eyes closed, I found myself staring at a poster of Cobain, crouched in foetal position around his guitar, head bent, face hidden under his mop of hair, as if he'd already crawled inside himself and disappeared.

Julie and Jim are coming for lunch today. I kept nagging Ma about inviting them. Then I just asked Julie, she said yes, and there's nothing Ma can do about it. We went to the bakery where I picked out a chocolate cake and some seven-grain bread because Julie eats healthy. I hope she likes tuna. If not, there's egg salad and a bottle of wine.

At twelve-fifteen, I ask Ma to take me next door to see what's keeping them, but she says, "Just wait. She's not the type to be on time."

Julie arrives at twelve-thirty without Jim. "He's got friends in from out of town. This looks delicious, Shel. Too bad I'm a vegetarian."

Ma gives Julie a look that says she'd like to dump the plate of sandwiches onto her head, but she unscrews the bottle and pours her a glass of yellow wine.

"Cool fish." Julie traces her finger across the glass tank.

"They don't like that," Ma says.

"They don't care," I say. "They don't have feelings like real pets."

Julie drinks three glasses of wine and eats some cake. A smudge of chocolate appears on her chin. My wine is watered down in a mug, but it still tastes good, and so does the cake Ma is feeding me in small forkfuls.

"Can I do that?" Julie asks.

Ma looks at her as if she has just sprouted wings and flown around the room, then shrugs, handing her the fork and plate.

"You have some chocolate on your face," Julie tells me.

"So do you." I laugh. Julie does too, her big deep laugh that makes you jump inside.

Ma grabs our empty plates. The hiss of water and clatter of dishes make it harder for Julie to understand me. "Say that again, Shel."

"I really want to hear you sing," I repeat.

"Sure. That would be great. I'd sing for you now, but I had a rough night, and my throat's a little sore."

"I want to hear you and Jim at the club where you play. I used to go to clubs. Now I don't go anywhere."

"Okay. We'll get Jim to ask your mom. She likes *him*."

Ma stands in the kitchen doorway, a dishtowel draped over one shoulder, both hands on her hips. "It's time for Michelle's nap," she says.

A rush of blood makes my face hot. "I'm not a baby!"

"I've got to go anyway," Julie says. "Don't forget our plan." She winks, gives my shoulder a squeeze.

I wish I could feel her hand there. "Don't go, Jule."

But she's out the door.

I remember bursting out the door of our grey house one afternoon, and waking in a white-sheeted hospital bed the next. The chrome bars on either side made me think of Zack's bike. The sharp smell of antiseptic burned my nose. Ma said I'd been in an accident. Her face told me that Zack was dead, but that

that didn't matter. What mattered was that I try to move my legs, my arms. I couldn't remember the accident—only Zack driving in the middle of the road, the screech of my voice.

Numbness, pain, heaviness, lightness, little flickers of pleasure floated over me like memories. I could see the distant white hills my toes made under the sheets, but I couldn't move them. My body was a television unplugged from the electricity of my brain—stranded, useless. Wires stuck to my chest and head with tape. A tube ran up my nose and down into my stomach, as if they were trying to plug me back in and hook me back together. When they poured yellow liquid through the tube, I thought of Zack filling his bike with gas.

Ma told me not to think about him, but she'd been telling me to forget Zack since we met, and when did I ever listen to her? I thought about the tangled blue sheets on his bed and the almost painful desire I felt when he used to drag his little finger across my belly, this way and that. I thought how he used to call me Shelley so I'd pretend to get angry and tickle him until he had to beg me to stop. I thought about the doughnut shop, the burnt taste of the coffee, the way the sugar from the crullers clung to my lips as Zack talked about the two of us moving to Vancouver where we could have the mountains and the sea.

When the nurse pulled the tube out, I could feel it wriggle through me like a chain rattling up inside my chest, neck, and face. Along with it came a secret thrill of relief, as if this might be it—they might finally be giving up on me. But they always shoved the tube back down again, scraping my raw throat, which was somehow full of feeling.

Another thing I thought about was the poster of Cobain disappearing into himself, how one of the things I'd lost in the accident, along with my voice, was the freedom to decide when I'd had enough, to pick up the thin sharp rectangle of a razor blade or unscrew the childproof lid on a bottle of pills.

Jim's at the door. He's talking to Ma. I hear his soft, gruff voice, "You could use a break, and she'll have fun. We'll take good care of her."

"She's dead weight out of that wheelchair."

"Don't worry. I'm pretty strong."

I want to yell—Where are we going? But then I think, maybe they're taking me to the club to hear Julie sing. I stare at the aquarium. The tetras' red tails flit across the tank.

"Where are we going?" I ask, as Jim pushes my chair along the sidewalk, and Julie strolls ahead, sunlight brightening her wild hair.

"We're going on an adventure." Her voice is light and bouncy.

"Not to the club?"

"Not today, Shel."

We stop beside a cedar hedge. My chest tightens as Julie disappears into the greenery. When Jim pushes my chair through a gap in the bushes, I see a path leading downhill into a grassy park full of trees and the shadows of trees. A little wooden bridge hugs the sound of rushing water. A sign warns, "Danger," but I'm not so much afraid as excited, although the two feelings take up the same space in my body, which has started to buzz and hum now that we've left the world of the street behind.

"I didn't know this place was here." I'm breathing hard as if I've been running.

"And it's only a ten-minute walk from the apartments," Jim says.

I wish I could see his face because his voice sounds like he's smiling, and I don't think I've ever seen him smile. His usual look is serious and attentive, as if it's all he can do to listen hard and think at the same time.

Julie sits cross-legged under a chestnut tree, waiting for us. Jim parks my chair in the sun and stretches out beside her. People jog by, pushing strollers, walking dogs. Robins hop around or scatter into the trees. Jim tugs at the spring grass, while Julie sticks dandelions into his hair and behind his ears, blowing the white seeds into his beard, turning it grey. In my wheelchair, wearing orthopaedic shoes, a cardigan, and a blanket draped over my legs, I look like an old lady, even though I'm younger than they are. A scream rises like a bird in my chest. I press my lips together to keep it inside.

I want to be Julie, to feel Jim's coarse beard and smooth skin against my fingertips. And to be Jim, the feathery seeds landing on my face, Julie's hands fluttering over my head, caressing my long, strong back.

"Some adventure." I spit the words.

"We're just getting started." Julie holds a dandelion puff to my lips. "Make a wish, Shel."

I take a deep breath, but the only wish I can think of is the impossible one.

"No!"

Julie stands up, brushes grass from her jeans.

"I want to go home."

"We're not going home," she says. "We're going across the river."

Jim's look of attention deepens.

"You'll have to carry Shel. She can't weigh much."

"The river's pretty full," he says.

She looks at him for what seems like an entire, long minute. "We'll have to take these off." She unlaces my shoes, unbuckles the straps that hold me into the chair. Jim leans over to scoop me out of it. In his arms, I feel small and light, not a dead weight at all. I imagine that I'm a maiden in an old movie being helped across a muddy stream or a bride carried over the threshold. Shivers of anticipation prickle my scalp and run down the stunned length of my flesh. Like the buzzing and humming I felt earlier, I can't tell if these feelings are coming from my body or my mind.

The river is white with foam, but Julie finds a flat spot where the water moves more slowly.

"Come on." She steps out onto a big shiny stone.

We follow. Jim's arms must be trembling because I can see my legs shake as we land on the first stone. If I could move, I might jostle him so that he'd drop me. If he does drop me, the current might sweep me away, or I might sink to the sandy bottom. The water looks just deep enough to swallow me and fill my lungs. I might not even try to struggle. I wonder if Julie knows that. But when we make it to the other side, and Jim sinks to the ground, letting me roll out of his arms onto the soft-looking earth, I feel shivery and bright. Julie lies down beside me and strokes the hair from my eyes. I wish I could feel her fingers brushing my skin, wish she would thread them through mine, wish she would kiss me and make my lips tingle. But she and Jim lie as still as I do, gazing up through the blossoming branches of trees into the pale blue above.

Jim's at the door talking to Ma again.

She says, "The last time I let the two of you take her out, you brought her home exhausted."

I can't hear what Jim says. He's probably hanging his head, remembering how he let Julie pressure him into carrying me across the river. On the way back, he lost his hold for a moment. I slipped down past the buttons of his jacket, but he grabbed me up into his arms again, keeping his footing on the wet stones.

Ma keeps saying no. I still can't hear Jim's words, but his voice has a gentle, persuasive rhythm.

Finally, Ma says, "Okay, but only because she's been bugging me about this ever since she met that Julie. You'd better come in and tell her."

"Julie's singing at the club tonight." Jim nods as he speaks. "She wants you to come. So, if it's okay, we'll pick you up at eight."

"Yes," I say.

Watching his long body lope away, my chest begins to hum.

At eight o'clock, I'm waiting in my denim jacket and the

Nirvana T-shirt Zack gave me, feeling a little like my old self, wondering if the buzz of energy around my heart means that my body is waking.

At eight thirty, the buzz has moved to my ears, making me feel dizzy.

When I ask Ma to take me next door, she says, "That Julie is not someone you can count on."

"Maybe something's wrong." The words squeak out of my throat.

Wheeling me into the hall, Ma knocks on their door, waits, then knocks again.

"Something must have happened," I say.

"Something always happens."

I take a deep breath. "I'm going to wait out here."

Ma rolls her eyes, but leaves me in the hall until I start yelling to know the time. It feels like midnight, but it's only nine o'clock when she parks me in the living room where I can watch the clock on the old VCR.

At nine-thirty, my chest bones feel like they might snap. The tetras dart between their four glass walls. Julie could be lying dead, or fractured and comatose, stranded and crushed. But maybe Ma is right, and she has only forgotten me.

Next morning, when Ma wheels me into the hall so she can vacuum, the air smells sour. Julie is crouched on the floor, vomit caught in the nest of hair hiding her face. Jim darts out of their apartment with a roll of paper towel, hunches down beside her.

"Come inside, Jule," he pleads, wiping her hair, her face. "Come on. It'll be okay."

"What do you know?" She leaps up, pounds her fists against his back.

Jim doesn't flinch, even when she kicks his shins with her pointy cowboy boot and screams, "I can take care of myself. I'm not a cripple!"

The word slams hot and rough against my face, like the road

when I went flying off Zack's bike. I close my eyes to make it go away, but it lurks in the dark under my eyelids, crouches inside my ears.

Julie sinks back to the floor.

Jim wraps an arm around her and raises her, helping her inside.

Ma rolls my chair back into our apartment where I watch the tetras for a while, my chest muffled and still. The fish seem slower and sparser than usual. When I count them, three are missing. Ma must have scooped up their limp bodies while I slept.

Later she turns on the TV to some old movie. Fred Astaire and Ginger Rogers dance in a nightclub while people laugh and drink martinis. I've seen it before. The TV sits on the counter that divides the kitchen from the living room where I sit. This way, I can watch both the movie and Ma, who is heating tomato soup and frying cheese sandwiches. She melts an ice cube in my soup so it won't burn my mouth. I drink it through a straw. She rips my sandwich into pieces, feeds them to me, one at a time. When she wipes my mouth and strokes my cheek, the warmth of the cloth makes the tears swim up, and Fred and Ginger look like they are dancing under water.

Peloton

JACK SLIDES AN ICE CUBE FROM HIS GLASS OF TEQUILA, RUBS IT over his hot, stubbly face and down his neck where it vanishes.

"Maybe we should get air-conditioning," he says.

"Can't take it?" Joanne asks. Her grin reveals the dark slit between her incisors that still turns him on.

To escape the fearsome heat upstairs, they've spent a week of nights lying naked on the living room floor on the futon from Joanne's daughter's old room.

Over their heads, the ceiling fan spins a frenzied blur. On the TV screen, cyclists in the final week of the Tour de France push up a winding road in the Pyrenees, which has its own history of border skirmishes.

"I want to quit teaching and live a year in France," Joanne says, eyes fixed on the racers.

Jack knows what Joanne wants. He keeps a list in his head, anxious to be the one to grant her wishes, but reluctant to satisfy all her longings in case she stops needing him.

When they bought the house twelve years ago, he said, "It doesn't have to have everything we want. A house can't make you happy."

"Some real estate agent." Joanne pressed a manicured finger against his breastbone. "Shouldn't you have faith in the dream you're selling?"

That was after their honeymoon in Europe. They'd followed the Rhine from Amsterdam to Alsace in a rented Saab convertible, her red hair a balmy, twisted flag, his eyes bloodshot behind fake Serengetis. Back home in Toronto, still living in Joanne's old fifth-floor apartment, the window air-conditioner chugging out noisy breaths of coolish air, they'd scanned the MLS listings, conjuring their future, inventing a list of what they wanted: three bedrooms—one each for his son and her daughter—, two bathrooms, a Jacuzzi tub, a private yard where they could drink wine on warm evenings as they'd done all through Germany and France, a garage for his aging BMW, gas heating, central air and central vac, hardwood floors. And a shorter list of what they couldn't do without and what they ended up getting: three bedrooms, two bathrooms, a yard.

Jack's boyhood house was a small two-storey brick like the one they lived in now—entrance to the side leading into a galley kitchen where his mother cooked dinner with a gin and tonic in one hand so she'd be able to work up a smile for his father. He was in sales too—Formica back then.

Joanne wants to redo the kitchen where the grey Formica is starting to buckle and peel, and the fridge stinks of limp celery no matter how feverishly she scrubs it. But she wants more to escape to France, to flee this sinking ship of a house, the paint blistering on the bathroom ceiling, the swollen window frames, the dank, spider-infested basement.

Jack watches her watch the peloton glide through France, trying to pin down her lust to one particular mountain, lake, or town. Her eyes narrow, her skin glows pinker whenever Kaz, the gifted young cyclist who's challenging the leaders, rides onto the screen, whenever the commentators sound the buzz of his name. There he is near the head of the peloton wearing the white jersey awarded to the best young rider. He squirts water in his face. Pedals spin under legs shaved smooth. When Kaz squeezes his eyes to sharpen the blur of the road ahead, Joanne bites her lower lip, filling the space between her teeth.

Jack starts a new list—the things they've denied themselves or each other: air conditioning, a Jacuzzi bathtub, a kitchen reno, anal sex, a really good screaming fight, a dog, TV in the bedroom, children together. The kids from their previous marriages have grown. Two worry lines ride Joanne's forehead whenever she thinks about Sophie in Montreal, sewing curtains and singing frantic songs.

"At least Aaron is settled," she says, looking away from an ad for some anti-anxiety drug with troubling side effects, continuing one of their on-going conversations that hang within reach like low wires crisscrossing.

"But he's too young to get married, and that damned bank works him too hard."

"At least when he marries, he'll move out of his mother's house." Joanne rests a hand over Jack's heart, aware of the burden she's accepted for keeping the pieces from flying apart.

When Jack's mother was drunk, she used to break her grandmother's Limoges cups and saucers, winging them over his head into the leaded windowpanes. He didn't know enough to duck. Instead, he marvelled at how the windows never cracked or chipped, simply flung back the bits of pink and white china. But later in bed, when he picked them from his hair, the sight of blood smudging his fingertips made his legs tremble.

Jack picks out Kaz and his teammates, all wearing red, from the mosaic of coloured jerseys. From behind, the peloton looks like a herd of goats ambling up a mountain, shoulders forward, flanks swaying, held together by an invisible bond, a glue stronger than the yellow goop with which Jack's mother, when sober, tried to mend the least damaged cups. Tension forms the peloton glue, tension between the comfort and safety of the pack, and each rider's longing to strike out on his own, casting off the ballast of the others' breath and sweat.

The housing market's been strong lately. But Jack has known years when he depended on Joanne's teacher's pay, when all that kept him going was the time he spent inside her, the memory of their last fuck, and the prospect of the next one, when he'd drive by the school just to make sure her red Honda was parked in the lot. One day it wasn't, but that evening she showed him two bandages on her back where the dermatologist had sliced out precancerous moles.

During the next round of ads, Joanne's head and shoulders slump against the base of the yellow love seat that's serving as their headboard.

"I feel nauseous," she says.

"I thought you liked the heat."

"But this is too much."

She rests a hand over the closed eye of her navel, lets her big toes fall together. Her chin seems to slide into her neck, as if all of her disappointments have hollowed her, but when the cyclists return, she raises her head, alert and taut once more.

The peloton splits and reforms like an amoeba. Kaz speeds up, starts to pull ahead, but something causes his bike to sway. It leans into the rider beside him. Jack hears the sharp pull of Joanne's breath, feels her holding it. The other rider wobbles, falls, skids to the side of the road, while Kaz stares ahead, willing his bike upright. Joanne breathes out. The commentators burst into speculation—a stone in the road, sand, bad luck, skittish nerves. The other rider picks himself up. His thigh is bleeding, but he's okay. They spray his cuts, bring him a new bike. All this takes no more than a minute before he's back in the race, chasing the peloton.

"I saw this part earlier," Joanne says. But it hasn't stopped her from watching as if it's her first time.

In the morning, they'll take in tomorrow's race live until Jack has to meet a client. Joanne has the month off and can watch all day. Some days she never gets dressed, never goes out. Jack likes to imagine her at home, naked, unseen, unknown to anyone but him, like a princess waiting in a castle for her lover to save her, like a nun before she pulls on her habit, or a whore in an Amsterdam window, her fragile toughness contained by the glass.

As a child, Jack used to mix the drinks that killed his mother. He'd slice the lime's green flesh, inhale the juniper fragrance of the gin, free the fizzy tonic from its bottle, then spin the ice around with a plastic stir stick, setting in motion a hypnotic dance of lime and ice. Her favourite drink was just another potion he assembled under her tutelage. She also taught him to make infusions from herbs she grew in the garden. They were meant to cure stomachache, depression, and rashes. He tried them all, but they never had any effect, unlike the snuck sips of gin that made him lightheaded and happy, that cast him into a deep sleep and woke him from heated dreams—his mother flying on a carpet of her own dark hair, brittle as a broom.

Space closes between the leaders and the peloton as they approach the final ten kilometres. The overall leader, the American who won yesterday's yellow jersey, keeps looking over his shoulder, as if he can feel Kaz gaining on him. Joanne has seen the end of the race and knows its outcome, but she's keeping quiet so Jack can enjoy the suspense. The truth is that he doesn't care who wins the day, as long as it isn't Kaz, as long as he doesn't pull some heroic feat in the last minute and suck Joanne into the TV like a slurp of victory champagne.

"Let's think about renovations," he says. "We can afford a nice kitchen now. Granite countertops. Stainless appliances."

Joanne says, "Let's think about selling. We don't need all this space now that the kids never visit."

Her willingness to jettison their house makes Jack's sweaty neck shiver. She could just as easily push him from the convertible to speed more quickly uphill, just as easily pull ahead on the stretch as Kaz is doing now, her heels in their black cycling shoes spinning like a hypnotist's watch, head bent over the handle bars, heart pumping. The dark spread of sweat on Kaz's white jersey makes Jack's patched heart tremble and his trembling thighs ache to keep up for as long as they can.

Some things he's never told Joanne: When he failed to see her red Honda in the school parking lot that day, he took a gulp of vodka from the flask in his glove box. He keeps a flask in his car for emergencies. When his father was away on sales trips, Jack's mother used to crawl into his bed, her soft breasts under their thin nightshirt pressed against his shoulder blades, her long legs wrapped around his shorter ones. She slept at once, but his erection kept him awake, even when he was quite small.

Something Joanne already knows: In Amsterdam, after a few hours in the coffee shops, she encouraged Jack to try one of the window whores, the French-looking one with the rough dark hair, black stilettos, and pink and white scarf. There were tiny raised welts on the backs of her thighs. Jack thought they were bug bites.

Later, when he told Joanne, she said, "Maybe she cuts herself." She said, "Now that you've sinned, I can too."

Now that Kaz has made his move, he rides like a demon, forging a canyon between himself and the herd. The two leaders in blue and green jerseys keep looking over their shoulders as if their gaze might ward him off, but their watchfulness only seems to spur him on. Kaz seizes the final stretch through town, his white jersey taking the finish line seconds before the blue and green.

Jack's forehead drops into his hands. Tears burn his throat. He feels Joanne's slick hand cup the back of his neck.

He used to hold the window whore against Joanne, resent her for tricking him by setting a test he'd be sure to fail, but maybe she'd simply been offering a gift, having seen that the girl was not just another pretty object in a window, but a pink and white memory Jack longed to chase time after. Then she'd masked her generosity to make him feel less mean, claiming tit for tat, a debt she has never called in, as far as he knows.

"This house is making me unhappy," Joanne says. "If we sell, we can invest the money and go to France for a year, then buy a condo downtown when the market's cooled."

Jack wants to say no, wants to keep denying her the things on his list of her longings, because that's the only power he's ever been able to wield. With his first wife too. And his son.

But denial has always flown back at him—useless, broken.

He raises his head and nods, transfixed by the image of Kaz sailing through the crowd, holding up two triumphant hands.

Outside of Yourself

"THEY CAN'T FIND ANY WEAPONS OF MASS DESTRUCTION."
Patti twists the phone cord around her hand. "It was all a story
to get in there."

"Oh dear." Patti's mother likes to believe in everyone's
good intentions. "When I was pregnant with you, I tried not
to listen to the news. Watergate, the oil crisis. They gave me
such heartburn."

"But women and children have been killed because of those
imaginary weapons." Patti doesn't mention that the first few
months of her pregnancy, she'd avoided the news too and
ordered Jeff not to talk about Iraq.

"Is Jeff still AWOL?"

"What do you mean AWOL? He's not in the army."

"You know what I mean, Patti."

"Well, he's not here much, and he missed my ultrasound last
week. And our first childbirth class."

"Give him time. He'll come round."

"The baby's due in six weeks."

"Why don't you stay with me? It's so hot in that apartment."

"I have to go, Mom."

Patti and Jeff rent the second and third floors of a house.
Their kitchen window looks out onto the roof of the main
floor apartment's covered deck and the small backyard that
no one ever uses. Patti wonders if her baby will play there next
spring, crawling through the dandelions. She opens the window
for a breeze. A fly buzzes in. The broken screen has yet to be

replaced after Jeff's attempt to squeeze inside when he locked himself out a few weeks ago. He'd climbed onto the roof of the deck and scrambled up the thick, old ivy, instead of ringing the doorbell and waking Patti. She'd heard rustling and scraping, and had crept into the kitchen with her cell phone, prepared either to see a raccoon or to dial 911. When she recognized the sleeve of Jeff's secondhand leather jacket coming through a rip in the screen, she'd considered making the call anyway. A midnight arrest might have shaken Jeff up, made him ache to be back home in their bed. And watching two cops shove him into a white car might have helped to soothe Patti's anger.

The air had been cool that night. Now the longed-for Toronto summer is trying too hard. The cloying July heat wears Patti out, while her restless son sets her belly twitching. She holds a hand there, trying to find a rhythm to the kicks, watches the fly settle on the windowsill and crawl along the rim of the small, two-handled silver cup her mother had found in a cupboard and brought over for the baby. The cup is engraved with an ornate version of Patti's initials.

She has been reading about the objects stolen from the National Museum in Iraq. Stolen or destroyed. Tablets engraved in ancient languages were smashed. Some recently discovered and not yet documented. Clues to the beginnings of civilization lost. She feels the same grief and dismay that sank through her chest when she'd heard about the Taliban toppling giant Buddhas. She tries to write about the lost artifacts for her dissertation on Objects and Desire, but so far all she has are questions. Why do we admire some forms of iconoclasm, but find others unthinkable? And how does an object inspire such devotion in some and such fear, hatred, or indifference in others?

Jeff can't look at the silver baby cup without saying, "I bet you never drank from that."

"It's symbolic," Patti says.

But their unborn child is not symbolic. The latest ultrasound revealed his knobby shoulders and the floating finger of his penis. Jeff hasn't seen the image. He doesn't want to believe in the baby except as an example of Patti's stubbornness. The condom had leaked, and her refusal to take birth-control pills or any other drugs unless absolutely necessary had always annoyed Jeff, who popped ibuprofen and muscle relaxants like candy to release his sore and twisted upper back.

When Patti learned she was pregnant, her body had felt more solid and real. So had the world. That's why she hadn't been able to listen to news about the U.S. preparing for war, about weapons lurking in a desert land, whose leader was being portrayed as both devil and clown. She'd sought refuge in her thesis, analysing the weapons and the inevitable war as object and desire in an attempt to neutralise them, but her ideas had seemed increasingly abstract and had caused the base of her skull to ache. The day Jeff told her that Canada had refused to join the invasion, she'd rested her head on the kitchen table and sobbed with relief. Finally able to turn on the news, she'd listened with gratitude to the sound clip of Chrétien's familiar raspy voice, admiring the note of anxious determination it struck.

For now all she can do is gather ammunition, like this piece about the stolen artifacts, data she can arrange and test once she is her old self again.

Her mother says that Patti will never be the same again, that motherhood changes you, but Patti tells herself that she is not her mother. She feels devoted to the idea of the baby, but the weight she has to carry and the pain under her ribs where he's been punching her are not endearing. Doesn't love require an object outside of yourself?

As Patti naps in the early afternoon, images of the lost artifacts float and twist through her mind—a worn and chipped Buddha, a stone mask of a woman's determined face, a yellowed carving of a lion attacking a man—while the baby floats and turns inside her uterus, waking her with another blow to the ribs.

Somewhere in the city, Jeff floats too, trying to find out what he wants or what he's capable of. He's teaching an outdoor art class in a park a mile or so north of their apartment. What Patti knows is that the class is one of a series of weeklong summer workshops that begin at nine and end at one. She knows this from the brochure she found on Jeff's desk. She also knows that Jeff doesn't come home until well after one o'clock.

Since he tells her nothing about his day, she imagines him in the freshly mown park with his watercolours, giving his students a demonstration on how to approach the landscape, then sending them off with their paints and folding chairs to various corners of the park and into the adjacent ravine, while he stays behind to fiddle with the painting he's begun, but will never complete. Later he goes looking for his students. Some will need more help than others. He'll find himself spending more and more time with two women who sit together in the ravine, their beach chairs facing the woods. Patti calls them Rhonda and Janine. They bring spiked punch in a big thermos and enough sandwiches to share with Jeff and anyone else who has forgotten or neglected to bring lunch. Both mothers with young children in the same summer camp, they always have to leave a few minutes early to make it home in time for the camp bus.

Patti has stopped asking Jeff where he goes, relying instead on the scenes in her head. Every night when he crawls into their bed, hugging the edge, she listens to his shallow breath deepen and feels a troubled rush of power, certain that if she were to touch him, even gently, he'd fall.

Awake from her nap, Patti drags herself off the bed, brushes her teeth and her long hair, thinning at the right temple. Only a few years ago, Jeff painted a series of portraits of Patti brushing her hair. He used to draw and paint her all the time—quick sketches, longer studies, and detailed oils for which she spent hours posing. Some of those portraits are sold, but most stand around the apartment, propped against walls, leaning against each other. Later, she'll take a look at them, but now she is desperate for a turkey sandwich from the diner on Yonge Street. The fierceness of her appetite shocks her. She used to go all day without eating, caught up in her work, feeling only the mildest of pangs.

The fly has settled on the lone peach in the fruit bowl. Patti brushes it off, washes the fruit, cuts out the bruises, and devours the peach over the sink, juice dripping down her wrist. Unappeased by this offering, her belly pulls her out the door, as she imagines her son will one day, taking her where he wants to go, showing her things she wouldn't notice on her own. Like the acid green moss that grows in the cracks between the sidewalk and the railway ties outlining the front lawn. Like the silence from the house next door, which usually resounds with piano music. Like the small roll of paper stuck in the piano teacher's wrought-iron fence. Patti put it there herself not long ago, wrote the words it conceals—"Life is a long caress that finally kills us."

It may have been something she'd heard in a dream. She often used to jot down notes for her thesis, but this one did not relate to her work. She'd found the paper in the pocket of her denim jumper one morning when she was walking to the subway. On impulse, she'd rolled it up tight and slid it inside one of the iron curlicues.

Passing the fence now, Patti touches the note. The contact sends a shiver through the narrow bones of her wrist and hand.

Lily watches Patti from her bedroom window. When she and Max first bought the house, Lily had loved that fancy iron fence, even though it had seemed meant for a much grander place, loved how it made their front yard, one block from busy Yonge, into a secluded garden. She still likes to sit on her front porch, almost hidden from the street by shrubs and vines that hush the noise of the city, but she has talked to Max about taking down the fence. It's rusty in places, the gate creaks, and it seems a kind of folly now, like music played on a sinking ship.

Lily has read Patti's note, rolled it back up like a cigar, and replaced it inside the iron circle. Was it meant for her? For Max? Maybe the curly-haired screenwriter wrote it. He walks past the house several times a day, pushing his daughters in their rumbling double stroller, sometimes getting to the coffee shop by himself in the evening, laptop in hand. Lily imagines him writing a love story for Patti, wedging brief installments between the iron posts.

Patti is pink-cheeked and graceful, carrying her unborn child as if it were weightless. Watching her, Lily feels the weight of her forty-eight years. Her own children, Beth and Emma, are living at opposite ends of the country, in Vancouver and Halifax, where they attend university and where both have found summer jobs. This morning, she had an e-mail from Emma:

Hi Mom. It's busy here at the hotel and they've begged me to work right up until September so I won't have time for a trip home after all. I'll try to make it for Thanksgiving. Don't worry about Beth. We talked last night. Emma XO

Lily wills herself not to think about Emma's e-mail, or Beth's silence, or the unanswered phone messages she has left them both. The worries and power struggles of motherhood sometimes feel like all she has left, habits she clings to, even though she knows they can only drive her daughters further away. Already their childhoods haunt the house, creating an audible hush, whole chords and phrases, essential notes vanished from the soundtrack of Lily's life. She tries not to wish them back. Instead she thinks of a man she met four years ago, remembers each particular of his body, a litany of comparisons she made between him and her husband—how his chest hairs were rusty while Max's were black, how two blond hairs grew out of a mole on his left shoulder where Max had a smooth hairless mole, how Becket was exactly her height, but Max had to bend his head to kiss her, how his mouth tasted salty, and Max's sweet. She remembers each meeting, most of them ending in Becket's tightly made bed, the air fragrant with their mingled sweat and the leafy vanilla scent of his cigars. Remembers waking from a brief post-coital doze, wiggling her toes under the unyielding sheet where they met Becket's hairy ankle. She leaned into him, kissed the slope of his shoulder, but he didn't wake.

She wriggled out of bed, leaving the sheets intact, folded and tucked under the heavy mattress. Becket shared a house-keeper with one of the other condo owners. Mrs. Santos came for two or three hours every morning while he was at work, cleaned the apartment, made the bed, washed and ironed his clothes, and cooked his dinner, which she left in a glass dish in the fridge.

"What's she like?" Lily had asked earlier when he'd claimed that he wasn't a neat freak, that Mrs. Santos was responsible for the spotlessness of his rooms.

"I never see her." He'd nuzzled Lily's neck. "I just leave a check on the counter."

"You must have met when you hired her, when you gave her a key."

Lily had always longed for a Mrs. Santos, but had never been able to let go of the control she gained from those daily rites. They'd seemed to bind her closer to Max and the girls. Like Mrs. Santos, she prepared dinner early and unseen, before her daughters came home from school, and her students began to arrive for their piano lessons, long before Max returned from the suburban industrial block where he designed houses and shop displays, and oversaw the building of cupboards and counters in the huge dusty workshop behind his office.

"I left the key with my neighbour," Becket had said. "But she was here once when I came home to change for golf. She dropped the vacuum nozzle on my toe and muttered something in Portuguese."

"So?"

"So...she's short and matronly, and an excellent housekeeper, not a gorgeous pony like you."

"I'm not jealous, only curious. You shouldn't take her for granted."

"Are you kidding? Every night I kiss the clean counter and the casserole in the fridge."

"Good." Lily had kissed his nose, twining her right leg around his left one.

It was Friday afternoon, and Mrs. Santos was long gone. Naked and thirsty, Lily tiptoed to the kitchen and gulped ice water from the tap in the fridge door.

She hadn't known she was lonely until the September evening when the phone rang while she was folding Emma's and Beth's T-shirts and jeans. They'd been more than old enough to do their own laundry, but between homework, hockey, ballet, and basketball, they simply hadn't had time. Lily usually slammed the phone on solicitations, but when a clear, fine baritone had said, "Lilian Vance, I have the answers to all of your questions," she'd found herself swallowing the words, surprised at how smoothly they went down.

"Yes," she'd said. "I want to come to your seminar on mutual funds."

Her grandmother had left her and her sister Judith a little money. Lily had sequestered hers in a savings account at a different bank from the one she and Max used. Waiting to decide what to do with it, she'd fantasized about a baby grand, about trips to Barcelona and Venice, but nothing had felt pressing enough to dislodge the money. It was a life raft stowed, waiting for the right need to arise.

"You need to put your money to work for you," Becket told Lily and the dozen other people at the seminar. They were all older than she, most in their sixties. Becket was her age, her colouring, her height, but solid not lanky. When he gripped her hand, their eyes seemed to slide into each other, and she had to look away.

"Our technology fund is growing like wildfire," he said. "It showed a thirty-percent increase last year, and this year has almost doubled so far. This is an opportunity you don't want to miss."

"It's too risky for us," said an owl-eyed woman whose husband sat nodding his head.

"If you can't tolerate much risk, we have a nice dividend fund, mostly blue-chip companies. Your money won't grow as quickly, but you can't go wrong with it. The longer you hold it, the better it gets."

Lily wanted to hold him tight against her chest, firmly in her hand. I can't go wrong, she thought, transferring her money to Becket's investment company, one half into the dividend fund, the other into the swelling technology fund. When he shook her hand, she kept her eyes fixed on his until he asked her to lunch—Chinese food and beer. She joked about the cheapness of the meal.

"You're not a big client," he said. "Just an attractive one."

"How attractive?" Lily drank her Tsing Tao straight from the bottle, lips lingering on the glass edge.

He gripped her hand for the third time then, but didn't let go.

She never doubted the rightness of her and Becket back then. It was 1999. The tech fund was soaring, the dividend fund chugging along. Millennial anxiety made it seem okay, necessary even, to grab whatever you could get. Their third lunch spilled over into his condo two blocks from the refurbished diner where they'd eaten. His fingers were tough but smooth on her skin, as if he had no prints to leave.

When Max pulled her close the next morning, his sandpaper hands startled her. She was confounded by the excitement she felt at the contrast, as if Becket's smooth fingers were the bass line needed to make Max's tenor sing.

A fan hums behind Patti, shifting the heavy air of the diner. Even at two in the afternoon, all the booths are full, leaving a small table at the back where she waits for her lunch. When Jeff glides through the door, she opens her mouth to call to him, but the clatter and buzz of the diner and the distance between the two of them discourage her from really trying to make herself heard. Instead she watches him take a seat at the counter and stare at the familiar menu as if he's never seen it before. The waitress's approach seems to startle him, but he still manages to give her the self-conscious half smile that used to make Patti want to kiss the corners of his mouth.

He looks towards and away from the teenaged girls drinking coffee beside him. Patti can feel him notice their silky hair, the soft skin of their bare shoulders, their exposed lower backs where their T-shirts ride up from low-slung capris. Can feel it like the point of a very sharp knife dragged across her belly, making her breath shallow and the soles of her feet go numb.

She blushes at the thought that someone she knows might see her sitting here alone at the back of the diner while Jeff sits with the two girls at the counter. How strange that person would find it. The person she thinks of is her thesis advisor, Evelyn, a second-wave feminist for whom Patti strives to maintain a persona of independence, ambition, and control. How would Evelyn interpret her behaviour, her choice not to reveal her presence, to spy on Jeff like a neurotic housewife?

The waitress brings her an open-faced turkey sandwich glistening with brown gravy. She forgets about Jeff as she eats and is genuinely surprised to see him walking towards her on his way to the washroom.

"Didn't you see me come in?" he asks.

She refuses to lie, having promised herself that she will never be like her mother, inventing stories for her father about what things cost, how she'd spent her day, how the kids were doing at school, always smoothing out the wrinkles.

"So why sit here by yourself?"

"I didn't think you wanted me."

"Of course I'd want you," he says.

She licks the gravy from her fork.

He jiggles one heel against the floor. "Just a minute. I have to pee."

When he returns, he sits opposite Patti, who has finished her sandwich and ordered dessert. The waitress brings him an omelet and coffee while Patti notices the other diners, secure in their booths—old couples as silent as she and Jeff, young couples laughing and flirting, a single older woman in an elegant straw hat, her back to Patti. The angle of the hat suggests that the woman is enjoying herself. Her shoulders look relaxed and easy inside her cotton blouse, as if they've shed some long burden they'll never take up again. Patti thinks about the giant Buddhas, the elation the rebels must have felt when those old stones shifted and fell.

"How are you feeling?" Jeff asks.

"Tired and hot."

"Were you able to do any work?"

She stares at him—his face damp with sweat, his forehead creased, as it always is when his back is aching. It's been weeks since he last asked how she was. She discovers the anger rolled tight under her breastbone. "I think you should move out."

Jeff gazes at his empty plate. "How would you manage?"

"The way I'm managing now. If you don't want this baby, and you don't want me, what are you hanging around for?"

"I do want you, but you're not making it easy."

"You don't want the baby. And that's how I come now. We're a package."

His thick hair is stuck to his forehead, unbudged by the air from the fan. "I don't know. Maybe it will be fine, and I'll feel fatherly. I don't know. Right now I can't imagine it." He reaches for the back of his neck.

The waitress brings Patti's rice pudding, which she consumes slowly, Jeff watching. She doesn't look at him until she's done.

"Are you coming?" she asks.

"Later," he says.

Lily hasn't been out of the house in days. It's been even longer since she's driven her car, a '97 Volvo station wagon. Now that she doesn't need it to drive Beth and Emma, it sits in the ramshackle garage behind the house for weeks at a time. Their house is so close to shops and the subway that she hardly needs a car. The last time she took it out was to buy bulk packages of toilet paper and laundry detergent. But now she's discovered Internet shopping.

She doesn't exactly lie to Max about this new activity, but she doesn't tell him about it either, and he hasn't mentioned the empty courier boxes. He's overseeing three kitchen renos and the construction of a sushi restaurant, and Evan, his boss and business partner, has just promised to build a spa for a small in-town hotel.

Most nights, Max and Lily sit silent over a late dinner of scrambled eggs, or he grabs a burger between worksites, arriving home to find her soaking in the tub while Leonard Cohen's baritone rumbles like an earthquake through the house, and another courier box lies flattened in the recycle bin.

This afternoon when the doorbell rings, Lily knows it will be more stuff—pants or shoes she'll have to return because they don't fit, embroidered silk pillows, yoga blocks, low-mercury canned tuna, new and used books, so many books she can't read them all, so many she's had to order a bamboo shelf to stack them on.

"Sign here," the courier says.

Lily signs, accepting the white cardboard box. Inside layers of paper rest black stretch capris and a purple T-shirt with "Namaste" printed on the back in small white letters. Over the years, she has signed up for various summer activities—art workshops like the one their neighbour Jeff is teaching, a hiking group, a theatre club, yoga this year—but her attendance has never been good.

Summers stall and stagnate without the regular work of teaching, Max always extra busy, and now her daughters gone too. Last summer they were home: Emma scooped ice cream a few blocks away while Beth answered the phone in

Max's office. Still Lily hadn't seen much of them, since they'd spent most of their free time with friends, but there had been moments—midnight tea in the kitchen with Emma confiding her doubts about going away to Halifax, a Sunday afternoon watching *The Wizard of Oz* with Beth, who'd stretched out on the couch, resting her head on Lily's lap.

Lily hasn't been to yoga in three weeks, but she could go this afternoon. The studio is just a ten-minute walk up the street. Maybe a shower will give her the momentum she needs.

The warm water softens her pent shoulders, the gripped muscles of her scalp. As her jaw drops, tears mix with the water running down her face. She has missed two periods, hardly sleeps, has lost her appetite for food and sex, is losing herself, becoming someone else, someone older, old. But her usually thin body feels more solid, and she's developed a small belly, which refuses to disappear even when she forgets to eat. It sits in front of her like a Buddha, ready to lead or accompany her somewhere. She places a hand on it. It is tender and tough. I love you, she says, to no one at all, an old habit. But who does she love? And what does it mean? How will it help her? I need help, she tells the showerhead.

"You need to see a doctor," Max had said.

She'd promised to make an appointment, but that was last week. She won't take hormones so what's the point? It's 2003. The latest research on HRT has shown that it increases the risk of heart disease, and having had to visit both her parents in the cardiac ward over the past few years, Lily has a rational fear of heart failure.

She has already ordered ginseng, black cohosh, and chaste tree berry from the Internet, but they don't seem to be working, except that she feels very chaste since she is too listless, and Max too busy, for sex. Maybe her yoga teacher knows something that will help. Lily has paid for ten classes, but has only been to one. They did four rounds of sun salutation, then balanced on their tailbones in the boat, which set every muscle in her body quivering. While the others stayed in the pose, she let her head, shoulders, and legs drop. The teacher's repeated mantra, "Everything depends on the strength of your core," made Lily feel undisciplined and weak.

Patti is relieved to turn onto her shady street. The heat is a noisome burden like her desire for Jeff. If she didn't have this life inside her, these hormones making her weepy and vulnerable, she could be happy alone, writing her dissertation. But the larger the baby grows, the smaller she feels—a tiny woman with a belly out to there. Staring down at its unavoidable roundness, she doesn't notice the sparrows in the lilac bush until they flash in front of her. They seem to have burst from her belly like blackbirds from a pie. Just two years ago, she'd run a marathon, training with a group of runners who met in the ravine. Pure muscle and movement, she'd felt in control, invincible, her mind and senses invigorated. Now she is Thumbelina dodging the sharp beaks of birds.

After their first few meetings, Lily and Becket switched from Fridays to Saturdays because Becket could no longer spare time from the office.

One Saturday, Lily crawled out of bed, searching for a snack. She unearthed a red delicious from the pile of grapefruits in the fridge drawer, but it tasted pulpy. She threw it into the garbage under the sink. She'd told Max she was going to the movies with a friend and might stay out for an early dinner after the matinée. Now she felt the first tug of guilt as if a string had been looped and knotted around the muscle joining her neck and shoulders, trussing her like the Cornish hens she used to roast Saturday nights when Beth and Emma still went to bed early, allowing her and Max a peaceful late dinner. Now that they were in their teens, Friday and Saturday nights had become about driving them to friends' houses, dances, or the movies, then watching videos and drinking black tea until it was time to fetch them home again.

Lily held out both hands as if weighing on one the new and delicious thrill of eating pizza in bed with Becket, and on the other the known but heady pleasure of listening to her daughters gossip with their friends in the car, revealing secrets she would not otherwise hear, as the girls teased Beth about her crush on the drama teacher or Emma about her first kiss.

Lily climbed back into bed, pressing her cool skin against Becket's warm body.

He pulled her to him, murmuring, "Our children will have your eyes, your pony legs."

The muscles between her neck and shoulders squeezed tighter.

"If you want children, why haven't you married?" She was up on her elbow now.

"I wasn't ready."

"So when did you decide?"

"Just now." He was on his back, staring at the ceiling. "I dreamed we were in bed on a Sunday morning, you nursing the baby, me kissing the top of her head, our son dragging in a big stuffed rabbit." He turned to face her. His smooth fingers reached for her arm.

"It was just a dream," she said.

"It's gone now," he agreed. But the dream seemed to linger in the parched air like the vanilla scent of the cigars he smoked when she wasn't there.

Lily didn't stay for dinner, but came back when she could. Telling Max she'd signed up for a Pilates class Saturday mornings, she was in Becket's bed by nine thirty, home by noon. She tried not to ask why she needed Becket in her life, what kind of balance his love restored, because she could not imagine her weeks without him. She seemed to have become a new person, unruffled by her students' fumbling, more patient and easy with her daughters, letting Emma go to a party at a boy's house, as long as she didn't stay too late, agreeing to take Beth clothes shopping Saturday afternoon, but not too early.

Max said, "You look terrific in that dress. Must be those Pilates classes."

It was February, and they were on their way to a dinner party to celebrate Max's sister's twentieth anniversary.

He lifted Lily's hand, kissing it.

Her skin felt warm and prickly. Max wasn't one for compliments or hand kissing. His brusque manners were a family joke. At work, Evan was the front man, charming clients, making his rounds in a crimson SUV emblazoned with the company logo.

"What do you want to do for *our* anniversary?" Max asked.

"I'll have to think about it," she said.

"I thought a trip. Maybe Italy or Eastern Europe. Terrific architecture in Prague."

Lily thought of Becket's ears, how they clung to his bullet-shaped head beneath his cropped, lambs-wool hair, how she had never sat beside him in a car or on a plane, his head parallel to hers, listening to the silent percussion of each other's eardrums.

"I've started seeing a woman," Becket said softly.

So softly she could almost imagine he hadn't said it. They'd just kissed goodbye at his door, his bare feet on one side of the threshold, her running shoes on the other.

"What am I?" she asked.

"You're a wife. Someone else's wife. I just wanted to let you know so you wouldn't think you're the only one."

"I know it's not fair," she whispered, index finger tapping the doorframe. "But I *want* to be the only one."

Another Saturday, when Becket started to reminisce about how they'd met, the nostalgia in his voice caused Lily to shiver and pull up the blanket. From the bed, she could see her white runners lined up beside the door.

"Maybe I should take Pilates for real. Maybe that's all this has been, exercise."

"Not for me." He slipped one hand under the arch of her neck.

"So, how are things going with what's-her-name?"

"Things are going, but I don't want to talk about it. We never talk about Max."

"When you're married, will you want a mistress?" she asked, searching his face for the real answer.

"The tech bubble is going to burst," he said. "The NASDAQ is already showing a decline. The writing's on the wall. I think we should transfer all your money to the dividend fund." His eyes had their urgent, steamroller look.

"Okay," she agreed, closing his lids with two gentle thumbs.

Outside Becket's condo, the March sun warmed Lily's skin. The air smelled earthy and fresh. She couldn't bring herself to follow the slick, muddy stairs into the subway, which would have taken her home in fifteen minutes. Instead she walked up Yonge, the longest street in the world, imagining Mrs. Santos on Monday, changing the sheets, washing away the dried evidence of Lily and Becket's lovemaking, wiping Lily's fingerprints off taps and doorknobs, vacuuming up all traces of her dead skin cells and hair. The invisible Mrs. Santos making Lily disappear.

Lily dragged her sorry body past Beth and Emma's high school, where both girls were practicing for the school play. The house would be quiet when she got home. She wanted to keep walking, to leave the city behind, but by the time she reached her street, her clothes were damp with sweat, and her hips and knees ached. Just as she lifted the latch of the iron fence, Max's van pulled up to the sidewalk.

He called out, "Must have been some exercise class."

Inside the house, he said, "We have to talk about our trip." He was pinching his bottom lip between thumb and forefinger, a sure sign of stress.

Max had been planning their anniversary trip for May, but now he didn't know when he'd be able to go. "Evan's lined up too many jobs for spring and summer," he told her over the ham and cheese sandwiches he'd made while she was in the shower. "Don't look so upset. I promise we'll get there."

Lily picked the cheese out of her sandwich, abashed at her

good luck in the timing of Max's confession, but unable to stop her tears. She wept on and off for the next three days, Max's sheepish attentions making her even sadder and more contrite. She'd failed at love, not only with Becket, but with Max, Beth, and Emma, stealing time from them, hoarding parts of herself away.

That spring, she gave her students extra work, scribbled in their practice books with red marker, and pushed them to master their recital pieces to do well on the June exams. She flew at the piano, banging out Schubert and Beethoven, until Beth and Emma screamed at her to stop.

In September, prices on the Toronto Stock Exchange began to tumble, technology stocks leading the way. Becket had transferred her money as promised, but even the dividend fund was losing ground. People were scrambling out of the market, but Lily remembered what he'd said about the fund, "The longer you hold it, the better it gets."

In October, Max and Lily finally went to Prague and Venice. Her sister Judith drove in from Kingston to stay with the girls.

On the plane, she stared at the dark hairs sprouting from Max's ears, then slipped a quilted eye mask over her face. She seemed to sleepwalk through the five days in Prague while he pointed out arched windows, spires, pilasters, and pediments. Jetlag, grief, or allergies made her face puffy, her ears crackle. But the first morning in Venice, she woke to see her skin reflected clear and golden in the ornately framed mirror. She and Max made love in the canopied bed. Later, they stepped down streets glistening with receding water and consumed fragrant linguine and rosé in a small room crowded by six white-cloaked tables. Across the canal, orange asters spilled from window boxes, a fresco was peeling from a yellow wall, and three doves sat on a shining roof.

Wherever they turned, whichever alley they ventured down, they saw or heard something beautiful that made any ugliness around it beautiful too. "Look at that," Max said. A painting of a saint with golden eyes and alabaster cheeks hung beside the broken exit sign at an art gallery. "And those," she said. Dainty purple blossoms sprouted from mud in the cracks of the dirty sidewalk. They saw a glass and silver chalice fill with green light from the narrow stained-glass windows in a musty, sewer-smelling church, and heard a grey man caress a Puccini aria from a scratched and dingy violin while they watched the purple hole, where his nose should have been, open and close with his breath.

On the plane home, Lily leaned in and traced the curves of Max's ear, allowing her fingertip to brush the bristly hairs.

Patti drags her fingers across the iron railings of her neighbour's fence just as the piano teacher opens the door and peers out. Patti says hello, wishing she could remember the woman's name. For years, she managed to avoid the neighbours, but once her pregnancy became obvious, everyone on the street began to claim her. Even the reclusive piano teacher has asked when she's due.

Inside the apartment, Patti heads for Jeff's studio, where she examines his empty easel, his cluttered desk, the canvases stacked and lined against the walls, the window facing the piano teacher's like two eyes opening onto each other. The room across the way is empty except for a black upright piano, a few chairs, and a small desk. The piano isn't furniture, Patti thinks. Or art. It's an object used to make art, like a paintbrush, but it doesn't require paint, only a musician to press her fingers to its keys. Unless someone makes a recording to capture its movement through time, no evidence of the music remains, nothing to admire or lust after, nothing to denigrate or destroy.

She turns from the window and flips through the canvases, looking for her own image. She finds the piano teacher's back, supple as a question mark in its close-fitting black sweater, posed beside a boy with a shock of golden hair, the white of his shirt split into vertical lines of grey, purple, and yellow.

Under this painting is one of Patti in profile before she became pregnant. Her hair is a dark sheet of purple, black, and blue, lit with strokes of pure white, her face a swerving black line and pink smudge, her eye a white triangle edged on one side in brown and on the others with black. The predominance of white makes her eye appear to be looking away, at something the artist cannot see.

Tomorrow will be the final day of Jeff's weeklong workshop. Patti imagines the sunny weather giving way to drizzle halfway through the morning. When Jeff goes in search of his students, it will begin to pour. He'll find everyone in their usual places, packing up their paints, trying to keep their just-begun paintings dry. He'll direct them to a shelter at one end of the park while he searches for Rhonda and Janine, his shirt sticking to his chest, running shoes slipping on the muddy slope of the ravine. Thinking he hears voices in the woods, he'll follow a path that snakes through the trees and find their thermos in a clearing beside the riverbank, along with their folded clothes. He'll hear laughter, catch a glimpse of naked flesh swaying under water.

"Come in and join us," Rhonda will call, popping up from the river to show her big white breasts, while Janine dives under. Rhonda, uncovered, is as pale and round as the mushrooms that will sprout there after the rain. Although Jeff has spent a week wanting to lose his face in her dense, springy red hair, and his hands under her body-hugging T-shirt, what he'll want most now is to turn and run.

Later, he'll come home, having forgotten his talk with Patti in the diner. He won't expect to find a suitcase in the hallway or Patti's mother in the kitchen, wrapping the dishes in newspaper and packing them into a cardboard box.

He'll rush upstairs to Patti's office, where she'll be kneeling on the floor, sorting books and papers into a plastic bin, hair tucked behind one ear and falling over her shoulders. He has a sketch of her exactly like that, her profile with that same determined expression. He'll tumble back into that time when he wanted to capture her every mood and pose, when he explored her with a seemingly endless curiosity.

"Don't go," he'll say.

Patti pulls the painting from the stack, carries it to the bedroom where another portrait hangs over the bed. In this one, she gazes softly at the artist while holding three white-tipped fingers against her pink neck. An image can become oppressive, desire and possession holding the subject forever in check, stopping time, denying change. She'd read that Buddhist monks built elaborate sculptures out of sand to remind themselves of the impermanence of everything, knowing that soon the rising tide would wash their efforts away. So wasn't it fitting for a tide of reactionaries to topple the Buddha statues?

Patti takes down the pink and white canvas. She doesn't destroy it, simply replaces it with the purple and black painting, then turns the softly gazing Patti to the wall.

Lily doesn't make it to yoga. Instead she looks at old photo albums, dragging them onto the shady front porch because the air-conditioner has conked out, and the house feels unbearable. Max has promised to send one of his men to fix it, but Lily knows not to expect anyone. They're all too busy with paying jobs. She's given up asking for a new kitchen or bathroom. For years Max has talked about knocking down this house and building a bigger, better place, while time has stolen by, asserting its own work order of changes.

In the first album, Beth is a thoughtful, shiny-haired toddler, Emma an awestruck, bald-headed baby. Both stare at the camera and the woman behind it.

Becket has a daughter. Lily saw them one Saturday afternoon a month and a half ago outside the Royal Conservatory of Music, where she'd been adjudicating piano exams. He was bent over a stroller giving the toddler a spoonful of ice cream, but she'd recognized his smooth woolly head, his small, close ears.

She'd placed a hand on his shoulder.

He'd turned, rising awkwardly, pulling her in for a hug.

He no longer smelled of cigars, but his hands still glided tough and smooth against her bare arms and the blouse covering her back. Lily shivered as his ear brushed hers. Max was so much taller.

"Who's this?" she asked when they'd released each other.

"Rose." He wiped ice cream from the toddler's chin. "We've been to see the dinosaurs."

"She looks like me," Lily said.

Now, closing the album, she wonders if the baby she'd miscarried would have looked like Becket. She'd woken early one morning with gripping cramps and stumbled into the bathroom, locking the door. She'd sat on the toilet, arms folded over her knees, head down, struck numb by the metallic smell of her blood and the relentlessly regular pattern of the black and white floor tiles.

What Jeff had really wanted this morning was to lie flat on the grass to relieve his stiff, sore back, but instead he'd painted a brief, technical demo for his students, later making his rounds, giving pointers and praise, quelling the urge to rip their paintings in two. He knew that the rage gripping him was not about their efforts, or even their lack of self-consciousness, which he openly envied, but about his own fear and self-doubt. His failure to make a decent living, or to make a splash on the Toronto art scene, or even, lately, to make his wife happy seemed to foreshadow other failures—in marriage and fatherhood.

To shake off these thoughts and feelings he has to keep moving. Each day after class, he walks. Today, he walked homeward and stopped at the diner, but couldn't bring himself to return with Patti, where he'd hear more about his shortcomings as husband and soon-to-be father.

Now he heads through a string of parks and ravines to the

trail following the Don River downtown. At times the highway roars overhead. Other times he can hear the river like muffled music, like the piano teacher playing with her window closed. He walks for almost three hours until he finds himself on the beach skirting Lake Ontario.

The sun stands about two hours north of the horizon. He drops his backpack and crouches on the beach, hands cupping the sun-charged pebbles. Yesterday, Jeff had walked to the west end of the city and watched the ducks dive for food in Grenadier Pond, but this is better—the lake seems endless, the horizon a blur of washed-out cobalt and turquoise, the breeze a relief.

He hears the boardwalk shift under the feet of joggers, and a rustle and clatter further up the beach where a man stands by a tower of stones. One hand rests at shoulder height on his latest addition, waiting for it to settle. The stones are smooth and flattish, wider than the man's head. Other stone towers rise here and there, improbable constructs that look like they might fall over at any moment. Each stone could be one of Jeff's projects, ambitions, expectations—the juried shows, the artists' collective, the scant reviews, enthusiastic at first, but later cooling to lukewarm. Painting is considered quaint; film is the thing now, or multi-media installations, or encaustic, which he loathes for its resemblance to snot, shit, and other primal acts of self-expression.

He'd expected his life to be stacked shoulder height by now or at least up to his diaphragm. Not only his career but his marriage—Patti's life fitting perfectly with his, each of them clicking into place. Instead it feels like that messy pile of stones on the other side of the man's tower, the failed result of an earlier attempt.

Jeff longs to run down the rocky waterfront, a force of destruction and renewal, all the towers toppling behind him, all the stones rejoining the big pile that makes up the beach. But he finds an empty bench and watches the artist add to his stack, picking up prospects and weighing them in both hands. The man feels along their edges and their flat and bumpy sides, rejects one after the other until he finds one that might fit.

Maybe Jeff has simply not been working hard enough, has relied too much on others to buoy him up and carry him along—old teachers, other artists, gallery owners, and critics—blaming them for his failures, as if they owed him his chance, carrying grudges like the one he's been holding against Patti for getting pregnant, for refusing an abortion, for complicating his life, putting him in a position where he has to choose between boyhood and manhood, between going on as he has been with sporadic teaching jobs and the occasional show, or brushing up his resumé, trying for a more challenging position. Or working eight to ten hours a day in an art store or coffee shop while he comes up with a more inspired career plan. It might be a relief to pour lattes for a while, to watch the world wash up against his counter, its ebb and flow, its chatter and cravings. That would make a good subject—a series of paintings or photographs, image and text.

Jeff forgets about tipping over towers. Instead he pulls out his sketchbook, dashes off a few drawings, scribbles some notes. Looks up in awe as the beach rumbles and clatters to see the man's stack burst apart, the round flat stones bounce off one another, searching for new places to rest, the man's arm still held out at shoulder height, as if to measure everything he's lost.

It is less than two years since 9/11, and Jeff remembers staring up into an empty sky, convinced that the world had stopped, that nothing could make it start again. But soon planes had begun to fly, new buildings had been planned and constructed, babies had been born.

As Patti opens the front door, the curly-haired screenwriter strolls past without his kids, laptop slung over one shoulder. In the morning, she'd watched him push the double stroller, stopping to straighten the older girl's sun hat, bending to pick up the younger one's dropped sippy cup. She tries to imagine Jeff as a careful father.

Lily sits on the front porch in her new yoga clothes. The purple T-shirt hangs from her shoulders, but the pants hug her thighs like a fresh velvety skin. The mail carrier has just dropped an envelope into her hands, a statement from Becket's investment firm declaring that her money has doubled. She feels a sudden need to spend it, not on things but on travel, to move about in the world again. To stop sequestering herself.

She's still holding the statement when Patti appears at the gate with a large package wrapped in newspaper. Lily rushes to lift the iron latch and take the parcel from her arms.

"What's this?"

"It's you," Patti says. "Jeff painted it."

Lily props the painting against the porch rail. "Can I get you some iced tea?"

"Milk would be better."

Lily brings the milk. One day she might be a grandmother. It could happen quickly, shockingly. Will her daughters come back to her then, carting their babies, diaper bags, and bottles of expressed milk, expecting her to babysit, seeking her advice?

"Open it," Patti urges.

Lily loosens the tape, slips the paper from the canvas. Even though its subject is a naked woman seated at a piano, the painting is full of colour and flux. Her cast-off clothes lie crumpled and sinewy on the floor. Long swirling strokes of orange and turquoise compose her back and bottom. Her hair is a tight yellow coil. Her arms vibrate with echoing shadows that make them look like wings, trembling with inaudible sound. Her long splayed fingers seem to caress the length of the keyboard, as the black and white piano engulfs her.

"It's beautiful." Lily sets it down for a better look. She loves the colours, the shapes, her long serpentine back. It is music without time, frozen, and dropped into her hand like a curl of white paper.

"It's one of his best."

"But he doesn't want to give it away, does he?"

"He doesn't know what he wants."

Lily knows she should refuse the painting, but she doesn't want to. Looking at it gives her the same gleeful jolt she'd felt when she first peered into Becket's eyes—the heady, terrifying sense of being seen and known. Sometimes, playing the piano, she has felt that same recognition. Only then she was the one seeing and knowing herself, her naked emotions struck into sound, the air humming with her unashamed grief and joy.

"Thank you." Lily touches Patti's shoulder. "Let me know if there's anything you need for the baby. I have some stuff left from the girls."

As Patti walks away, Lily waves and keeps on waving, shaking out both hands. She hasn't played all week. She doesn't miss her students, but she misses the regular work of leading them through a piece. When she's not committed to sharing her love for music, she forgets it. Like playing the piano, love is a practice, a discipline. But when does discipline become punishment? The piano in the painting looks like it's about to cave in on Lily, and only the ceaseless movement of her arms and fingers can hold it back.

She couldn't have kept on loving Becket for long, not if it had meant neglecting Beth and Emma just when they'd wanted her least, but needed her most. That winter and spring after Venice when Beth was starving herself, locking herself in the bathroom after meals, refusing to speak to Lily, only to Max and Judith, who didn't ask questions. Or the next fall in the wake of 9/11, when Emma was breaking curfew with random boys, stumbling home numbed by cigarettes and beer, her lips red and swollen, bright eyes clouded. Lily had been unable to sleep then too, but most nights she'd managed not to yell at Emma, and sometimes even to listen to her stories.

Perhaps she hasn't failed at love after all. Lately, Max brings her tea in bed before he leaves for work. When she makes room for him to sit on the covers, he talks about cutting back his hours and building their dream house in the country. Lily hasn't dreamed in months. She wakes at three or four, damp with sweat, the night giving no clues to what she dreads or hopes for.

She has tried not to think about Emma's e-mail because she misses her daughters with a dull ache that begins low in her belly and trills out into every cell, a pain with its own inexplicable music. What she should have learned from loving Becket was how to let go. Instead she has been trying to hold on to everything and everyone, her hands and heart, her very blood, sluggish with fear and regret.

For now Beth and Emma have chosen distance, but Lily doesn't have to take that as a rejection. She doesn't have to punish herself. She can keep in touch, admit that she's learned more about love from her daughters than from anyone else. And when they happen to answer her calls, she can press the phone to her ear and listen, as if they were sitting right beside her.

Patti's mother brings cannelloni, cucumber salad, and an extra fan, which she trains on them while they eat. Patti tunes out the hum of the fan and the drone of her mother's voice, but she can't ignore the heat rash that flares along her skin or the fly circling her plate. Are the Buddhists right? Is it her desire for permanence that's making her unhappy? The stories she's been told about parenthood? The stories she tells herself? She can't confide in her mother, who would crow with delight, but she imagines telling her thesis advisor, Evelyn, about her longing for a stable marriage, a cozy traditional family for her son. She can almost see Evelyn's old ideas of her toppling, along with the pink and white Patti in Jeff's painting, and some of her own beliefs about Jeff and herself.

She doesn't want him to be an icon of the errant lover, or even of the perfect father, but only a real and separate person who will go with her to prenatal classes and hold her sweaty hand when she's in labour.

The story she will tell her growing son years later will unfold in his mind as a series of images—*Patti washes the dinner dishes with her mother, the kitchen window wide open to catch the evening breeze. The fly buzzes out as Jeff calls her name. His footsteps pound up the stairs. The baby turns inside her belly, pushing his fists against her full stomach, starting a wave of nausea. Her hand flies for the windowsill to steady herself. The silver cup she may never have drank from tumbles off, skips down the roof of the first floor deck, and lands with a clatter below.*

Acknowledgements

The following stories were previously published in magazines or anthologies:

"A Large Dark" in *Best Canadian Stories*
"Lemon Curl" in *Event*
"Unfinished" in *poem memoir story*
"Peloton" in *Room*

For assistance with these stories and support around their publication, I am grateful to Laurie Alberts, Mark and Meg Aubrey, Elaine Batcher, Shelly Catterson, Vivian Dorsel, Laurette Folk, Rilla Friesen, Abby Frucht, Jill Glass, Douglas Glover, Kristine Klement, Lisa Skoog de Lamas, Andrew Macrae, Dave Margoshes, K. D. Miller, Christopher Noel, Frank Tempone, Martha Wilson, and Eddy Yanofsky, with a special thank you to David Jauss for his generous and expert advice, and for his unwavering belief in these stories.

My literary communities have provided invaluable support and encouragement. Without them, the writing life would be much more lonely and a lot less fun. Thank you to the Summer Writers' Group, the Literary Lobster, Red Claw Press, *Numero Cinq*, the Saskatchewan Writers' Guild, Writers' Block West, Ve Shree, and to everyone who has taken part in Writers Workshop in Bermuda.

I am most grateful to the MFA in Writing Program at Vermont College of Fine Art, and to my workshop leaders and friends there.

A big thank you to all of my wonderful friends and family, and to Joseph, Kristine, and Kathryn, whose love continues to surprise and sustain me.

Kim Aubrey's stories, essays, and poems have appeared in journals and anthologies, including *Best Canadian Stories, Event, Numero Cinq, Room, The New Quarterly, upstreet*, and *How to Expect What You're Not Expecting: An Anthology of Pregnancy, Parenthood and Loss*. Kim has an MFA in Writing from Vermont College. She is Associate Fiction and Nonfiction Editor for *Grain* magazine, and a founding member and Editor of Red Claw Press. Kim grew up in Bermuda where she leads an annual writers' retreat. She currently lives in Saskatoon.